Once Upon a Time . . . Golden Threads

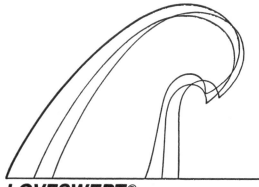

LOVESWEPT®

Kay Hooper

Once Upon a Time . . .

Golden Threads

Doubleday

NEW YORK · LONDON · TORONTO · SYDNEY · AUCKLAND

LOVESWEPT®

Published simultaneously in hardcover by Doubleday
and in paperback by Bantam which are divisions of
Bantam Doubleday Dell Publishing Group, Inc.,
666 Fifth Avenue, New York, New York 10103

LOVESWEPT, DOUBLEDAY and the portrayal of the wave device
are registered trademarks of
Bantam Doubleday Dell Publishing Group, Inc.

Library of Congress Cataloging-in-Publication Data
Hooper, Kay.
    Once upon a time—golden threads / by Kay Hooper. — 1st ed.
    p. cm.
    ISBN 0-385-26620-0
    I. Title.
PS3558.0587054   1989
813'.54—dc19   89-2304
                                    CIP

OG

For Carolyn,
Who's never daunted me by saying,
"You want to do *what*?"
Thanks.

AUTHOR'S NOTE

Any story idea usually comes to me in the shape of a very simple premise. "What if . . . ?" It may be a premise for a situation, an emotion, or a type of character. It may be all three.

What if . . . a young woman had been isolated through no fault of her own? What if she were rootless, cut off from her past and from all who had known her? What if she were trapped, imprisoned, but in a jail with no iron bars or stone walls?

Would she be like the innocent maiden in *Rapunzel*? Waiting with a kind of trusting patience for some prince to find his way into her lonely prison? Perhaps. All Rapunzel had to do was let down her hair and fall in love. But what if it were more complicated than that?

What if . . .

Once Upon a Time . . . Golden Threads

One

"Next!" Nick Rhodes glanced at the man sitting beside him and added in a much lower voice, "That makes eleven we've seen, and the last three could have—"

"No." The voice was deep, rich; the dark eyes twinkled gently in a benign face. "I haven't seen her yet."

Sighing, Nick nodded toward his assistant to bring the next potential Rapunzel onto the stage. He wanted to swear over the lengthy selection process, but the old man beside him possessed the trick of making those around him mind their tongues. Besides that, he was putting up the money for the play—which meant that he called the shots. Nick glanced at Cyrus Fortune again, thinking that he probably got chased down streets by children. Put him into a red suit, and he'd be the image of Santa Claus.

"This is a small town," Nick reminded Mr. Fortune. "Not many actresses to choose from, and half of them are completely wrong for the part. If we don't find her soon—"

"There she is." Mr. Fortune was gazing toward the stage. He was beaming happily. "There's our Rapunzel."

Nick's head swiveled toward the stage. He was prepared for almost anything, since Cyrus Fortune struck him as such an odd man. Now, seeing the young woman onstage, cautious relief was his strongest emotion. She waited somewhat nervously for instructions and could have been any age between twenty and thirty. She matched his mental vision of Rapunzel. She was petite, almost fragile, her pale gold hair pulled back from her face and held with a ribbon.

Nick studied her with the critical eye of a director. A lovely face, he decided judiciously. And there was something about her, a quality he could see or sense even from his seat in the empty, darkened auditorium. Wariness? A look of loneliness? His gut reaction was that she would know just how to play a forlorn maiden locked in a tower. If she could act, of course.

He leaned forward, propping his forearms on the seat in front of him. "What's your name?" he called.

"Lara." Her voice was soft but curiously clear and distinct, reaching him easily. "Lara Callahan."

"All right, Miss Callahan. If you'll read page twenty, please? Tim will cue you." He nodded toward his assistant. Then he settled back and listened as Rapunzel pleaded with the witch to allow her to go free. Lara Callahan's voice was sweet and unbearably sad, her plea so eloquent that Nick felt a feathery chill brush his spine.

Cyrus Fortune was nodding, beaming. Above the bushy white beard, his cheeks shone like polished apples. He was leaning forward slightly in his seat, his elegant hands resting on the gold-handled cane between his knees. "There," he said softly. "There."

There, indeed, Nick thought. He wondered why Lara Callahan had never auditioned for him before. Was she new to the relatively small town of Pinewood, Virginia?

"Fine, Miss Callahan," he called as soon as she had finished the scene. "Rehearsals start day after tomorrow. Monday, six P.M.."

She looked almost comically startled. "You mean I got the part?"

"Didn't you want it?" Nick laughed a little as Tim, clipboard in hand, led the bemused Rapunzel into the wings. "Tim," he called, "ask the crew to wait for a few minutes, will you?"

"Sure, boss," Tim replied.

Turning to face Mr. Fortune, Nick said, "The biggest part cast. Now we just have to worry about the parents and the witch."

"And the prince," Fortune reminded him.

Nick was conscious of his impatience, and tried to repress it. "Four actors showed up to audition for that part, and you dismissed all of them. We have to pick one of them—"

"You replaced the notice on the front of the building?"

"Yes," Nick admitted. "You told me to. But I don't see what you hope to gain by it. We ran a notice in the papers for three days setting today only for auditions. No one will wander in off the streets to read for the part, not this late."

"You never know," Cyrus Fortune murmured. "I'll make my decision by the end of the day. Have you assembled the stage crew?"

Nodding, Nick said, "Of course. Most of them are people I've used before, though I couldn't get my usual foreman. They're moonlighting, like the actors. Most of the sets will be built while we're rehearsing in the evenings, and on Saturdays. As usual. You've approved the set designs and the script; I have the costume sketches in my office, if—"

Cyrus Fortune heaved himself to his feet with a considerable effort. "Certainly, certainly." His voice was a gentle baritone. "Your wife is an excellent designer and seamstress, Nick. I'm sure I'll have no complaints."

Following the impressive bulk of his backer down the aisle toward the stage, Nick reflected that Susie had indeed done a fine job with the costume designs —but what was Fortune's knowledge of her reputation based on? Nick had certainly never heard of the man, not until he's appeared at this theater a few weeks before with a proposition. He would provide the financial backing for a production of *Rapunzel,* he'd said, with all profits going to local charities.

Rapunzel, of all things! Susie had been delighted by the opportunity to design romantic costumes for a fairy tale, but Nick had nearly torn his hair out over the script. He had persevered, mainly because his generous backer had made a large deposit to the theater's bank account and—except in the area of the principal players—was placidly uncritical and did not interfere.

And so, the Pinewood Community Theater was

due to stage a production of *Rapunzel* in less than a month.

Provided, of course, that a prince could be found. Nick hardly shared his backer's sublime belief in the intervention of providence to supply them with a suitable prince, but he was somehow unsurprised the following morning to look up from his desk at the sound of a knock—and behold Rapunzel's prince.

"Mr. Rhodes?"

"Yes?" Nick rose to his feet. "What can I do for you?"

"One of the workmen said to see you. Have you completed auditions for your play? I saw the notice out front."

Nick hoped that Fortune wasn't the type to say I told you so. "We have one part left," he admitted. "The prince." Nick half-expected this big, powerful-looking man to turn and leave, for he didn't seem the type to contemplate with anything but a sneer the idea of playing the role of a prince in a fairy tale.

"May I read for it?"

Nick decided that he was getting old; his intuition wasn't what it used to be. "Certainly," he murmured. And, again, he was unsurprised when Cyrus Fortune beamed happily upon seeing the dark prince.

"Now then," Fortune said softly, nodding. "Now then, we'll see."

Nick didn't have the nerve to ask what they would see.

On Monday evening, Lara sat on one side of the stage, not quite in the wings. She had meant to study the script, which she hadn't yet read since Nick had just handed her a complete copy, but found her fascinated attention on the stage crew milling about. What they were doing—hammering, bellowing at one another, carrying bits and pieces of lumber here and there—looked like total chaos, but she assumed there was a logical pattern to the activities. She reminded herself that there were at least three very different sets to be constructed, and wondered how on earth they could be built in the time available.

"You're sitting on our tree."

Startled, she blinked up at an extremely handsome masculine face in which blue eyes danced merrily. He was standing, hands on slim hips, directly in front of her.

"I beg your pardon?" she managed to say.

"Our tree." He gestured to the bogus log she had chosen to sit on. "I wouldn't bother you about it, but we're trying to build the garden first, and we need the tree."

Lara got up hastily. "Oh. Sorry."

"No problem." His deep voice was cheerful. "I'm Luke Brady, by the way, foreman of the stage crew."

"Lara Callahan," she said.

"I know. Rapunzel. Lovely golden hair and all."

"Are you sure your last name isn't Blarney?" she asked dryly.

He grinned. "I'm sure."

"But you *do* admit to being Irish?"

"Oh, of course. Would I be tryin' to deceive a fine Irish lass like yourself, darlin'?"

She couldn't help laughing; the brogue was marvelous. And with his flaming red hair and wicked

6

blue eyes, he had doubtless been a heartbreaker for years. "I wouldn't bet against the possibility," she told him.

Luke Brady assumed a wounded expression. "It's cruel you are," he said sadly.

"Luuuke!" one of the other men wailed desperately.

Moving quickly out of his way, Lara said, "You'd better get your tree before somebody over there has a fit."

Chuckling, he bent and got the tree, tucking it easily under one brawny arm. "I *am* the foreman, you know," he said, dispensing with the brogue. "If anybody has a fit, it's going to be me."

Lara watched him stroll back toward the other side of the stage, carrying the tree. She knew it was hollow, of course, little more than a shell with the appearance of solid wood, but he looked as though the real thing would have presented no problem.

"Lara?" Nick appeared from the wings, looking harassed. "We're going to try a read-through back-stage, so—" He broke off, staring across the stage, then yelled, "Luke! The tree's for the outside of the tower, not the garden!"

"Sorry," Luke called back, standing the tree on end and leaning it against the skeleton of a cottage. He sent Lara a wink.

She felt herself flush. Had it been an excuse to talk to her?

"Study the set designs, people," Nick requested in a voice that held despair. He took Lara by the arm and began drawing her backstage. "Half those guys don't know what they're doing," he said under his breath.

7

Lara glanced at him as they made their way through a tangle of ropes and electrical cords, props and lumber. He was a man somewhere in his forties with a salt-and-pepper beard and dark eyes; he was fast-moving and prone to get excited about things. Lara didn't know what kind of producer and director he'd be, but his script for the play was just beautiful, she thought. He had taken a brief fairy tale and fleshed it out, giving it humor and substance. She liked him for that alone.

"Here we are," he said briskly as they reached a long, scarred wooden table placed as far out of the path of chaos as possible. "You've met everybody, Lara, except for your prince. Lara Callahan—Devon Shane."

He's going to climb up a rope made of hair? was Lara's first thought, as the big, dark, coldly handsome man with brooding sapphire eyes rose politely from his chair.

"Hello, Lara," he said, studying her with a detachment that made her feel as if she'd been stripped naked, weighed and measured, and was about to be examined coolly under a stark fluorescent light.

"Hello," she murmured, taking the chair Nick indicated on the other side of the table from Devon. She felt wary, disturbed—and couldn't have said why, except for that dispassionate sapphire stare. She'd been instantly comfortable with everyone else she'd met since getting the part, but Devon Shane made her acutely *un*comfortable.

She eyed him cautiously as they got ready for the read-through of the script. Shane . . . another Irishman. But this one wasn't cheerful and fiery like

Luke; this man was Black Irish—a dark, brooding Celt, with all the signs of a dangerous temper only an insanely reckless person would willingly rouse. He was hardly the pretty, charming prince of fairy tales, despite being so handsome. Yet Lara knew this man would appeal to any woman far more than a bloodless fairy tale prince would.

They wanted happily ever after, Lara reflected of her own sex, but there was that part of every woman that longed wistfully to tame the heart of a savage man.

As for herself, Lara wanted nothing to do with savage men. She'd seen enough violence, too much. She wanted peace, wanted a normal life without the darkness of potential danger hovering over her like a vile shadow.

"All right," Nick said as his nervous hands smoothed open the plastic-bound script on the table before him. "Let's get started. Act One, Scene One . . ."

Lara paid little attention, since her own part didn't begin until the second act. Instead, trying to keep herself from becoming too absorbed with the danger-ous-looking man across the table, she studied the other players as they spoke their lines.

The parents of Rapunzel were played by Sonia and Pat Arnold, a couple in their thirties with an obvi-ous passion for amateur theater. Nick had explained that they often acted in the plays he produced, delighted merely to have minor roles. Sonia was a cheerful blonde with a trim figure, and Pat was a handsome man with a friendly smile and an amaz-ing baritone voice.

Melanie Stockton, a newcomer to the area, was

slated to play the witch. Melanie, with her black hair and exotically slanted brown eyes, had a deep and sultry voice that could sound utterly wicked. Nick had chosen her to play the part because he'd given the part a neat, modern-day twist—his witch wouldn't be an old crone, but a woman of evil glamour.

As for herself, Lara had no idea what she was doing in this theater. She had come to the audition on impulse. The walls of her apartment had been closing in on her, as they so often had these last months, and she had wanted badly to escape, to find something radically different for her life. She was tired of being alone, tired to being wary and afraid.

And here, in the midst of this noisy turbulence, she felt more alive than she had in a long time. She had never thought of herself as an actress and had been certain she'd suffer from stage fright, but from the moment she'd begun reading at the audition she had felt natural, comfortable. She hadn't been Lara Callahan; she'd been Rapunzel, alone and lonely. Pleading to be set free, to be allowed a life outside her dark tower.

Lara felt her lips twist as she silently admitted just how well the role fit. The difference lay only in Rapunzel's ability to plead her case; Lara had to bear her own isolation in silence, because no one could simply open a door and set her free. But at least she could pretend.

"Great, great," Nick was saying happily. "That was fine. Act Two, Scene One. Lara, can you sing?"

Turning the pages of her script to get to the right place, Lara said distractedly, "I don't know, Nick. I've never tried."

"Want to?"

"No."

He grinned at her. "Okay. I hadn't planned a song anyway. We'll use some kind of music to lure the prince, though. Do you play an instrument?"

"Piano."

"How well?"

Lara started to tell him she'd competed as a teenager, then remembered that it had been in her other life. A long time ago. She felt a flash of pain, but ignored it. "Well enough," she answered briefly.

Nick nodded and made a note on the legal pad lying beside his script. "We'll get a piano, then, and dress it up to look fancy. We'll decide on the right music later."

She half-nodded an agreement, and then a prickle of awareness made her glance across the table. Devon Shane's eyes were fixed on her face. Lara tried to look away, but she felt curiously trapped by his sapphire gaze, caught by something she couldn't define. For an instant she thought of the fascination people had with gems, with their coldly luminous glow. . . .

Then she realized that Devon's eyes were neither hard nor cold. They were bottomless, burdened eyes, filled with shades and shadows. She was conscious of a bone-deep ache, of something disconnected and alone and wary. It was a jolt, seeing those qualities in his eyes, an almost primitive shock of recognition and affinity.

"Lara? It's your line." Nick sounded impatient.

She broke Devon's steady gaze and stared down at the script. Her line. Rapunzel's line. In a voice that shook, Lara read, "Why may I not leave this place, Mother? I wish to—"

Melanie broke in with the voice of the witch, soothing and authoritative, her cold smile for the benefit of the audience rather than the trusting Rapunzel. "My child, the world outside this tower is a cruel place, and I would keep you safe from it. I will bring you a nice pet, shall I? You will have a companion when I leave each afternoon."

"Damn!" Nick muttered.

"I wasn't finished," Melanie told him in her own voice.

He shrugged apologetically, but said, "I just remembered how much trouble we had the last time we needed an animal. Maybe I can find a bird or something."

Lara was still trying to ignore the man across the table, and said almost absently, "We can use my cat."

Nick looked at her. "A cat? Lara, if your cat's anything like Susie's, it won't take kindly to stage direction."

"You don't know Ching."

"A Siamese?" Nick asked with foreboding.

She had to laugh. "Yes, but not—not at all catlike. I'll bring him in if you like, and you'll see what I mean."

"Worth a try," the director said. "Bring him in tomorrow night, will you? Okay, Melanie, go on."

Melanie went on with the witch's lines, and Lara concentrated carefully on following and reading hers. At this early stage they were just reading, occasionally trying a certain tone or inflection. Nick interrupted from time to time and suggested a slight change in wording or a different emphasis, and they all made notes right on the script.

Lara's concentration increased as the reading continued, until she was virtually unaware of the banging and thumps out on the stage; she didn't even notice when the workers packed up for the night and left. But when Devon Shane spoke his first line, her thoughts scattered like leaves blown by a wind. His earlier brief greeting hadn't prepared her for the effect of his voice. It was deep, compelling, curiously haunting; and the single, simple line he spoke was a plea that made her ache inside.

"Rapunzel, let down your hair. . . ." *Let me know you. Let me be with you. Let me love you.* It was all there, an appeal to break a woman's heart.

As Lara looked up from her script to stare across the table at him, she realized she wasn't the only one affected by that dark velvet charm. Both Melanie and Sonia were looking at Devon with a kind of unconscious fascination; Pat gazed at him in surprise; and Nick wore a peculiar expression of baffled delight.

"Good," he said blankly. And then, as Devon looked at him somewhat enigmatically and without comment, Nick added more briskly, "Very good. Now, I skimped on the stage direction at this point, but here's what I've planned. . . ."

What Nick had planned deviated slightly from the fairy tale. Rapunzel was trusting, he pointed out, but hardly an idiot and not at all deaf; she was bound to be able to differentiate between the prince's voice and the witch's. So he had decided that

Rapunzel would lean out the tower window to see who was calling to her rather than meekly lowering her braid. The first meeting between the potential lovers would take place with the prince still outside Rapunzel's stone prison.

They talked to each other, two lonely people. Rapunzel was innocent and curious, needing what she couldn't put a name to, and this prince, like all fairy-tale princes, was falling rapidly in love with her beauty and purity.

Lara spoke her lines, gazing steadfastly at her script and trying to ignore the effect Devon's husky voice was having on her senses. But as they progressed to the next scene, where the prince charmed Rapunzel into lowering her braid, Lara slowly realized that Nick had chosen to portray the lovers realistically. She remembered, now, that in at least one version of the fairy tale, Rapunzel had borne twins by the end of the story.

Nick, adapting the tale for what would be an audience made up of adults, had decided to focus on the developing relationship, building sensuality as well as love and tenderness between them. By the beginning of the third act, Rapunzel and her prince were lovers in every sense of the word.

There would be no nudity, but the embraces Nick described with enthusiasm were passionate and sensual in the extreme. It was not something Lara had been prepared for—fairy tales tended to limit sexuality to chaste kisses—and she wasn't sure how she felt about the matter. Nor was she able to guess how Devon felt about it, since the expression on his darkly handsome face remained enigmatic despite the emotion in his haunting prince's voice.

She heard her own voice quiver with uncertainty as they continued reading lines, and wondered what the others heard in it. Nick, at least, seemed wholly satisfied, even delighted.

He glanced at his watch as they finished the first scene of the third act, and pursed his lips thoughtfully. "It's after nine. I think we'll leave the rest until tomorrow. Is anybody going to have a problem showing up by six every night?" He looked around the table, then nodded. "Good. Okay, then, same time tomorrow. Take your scripts home and study them if you get the chance."

Lara gathered her script and rose, fighting a craven impulse to tell Nick he'd have to find another Rapunzel. She was, she reminded herself, a grown woman, and it was only a play, for heaven's sake. An adult version of Dress-up or Let's Pretend, with costumes and fake kisses. She could handle that. And she needed it, needed the focus in her life right now.

She'd been working sixteen hours a day for too long, exhausting herself just to be able to sleep without nightmares. When the inevitable crash had come, weeks ago, it had left her limp and unable to work; the walls had started closing in on her, and she'd wanted to run—somewhere. Anywhere.

Anywhere except home. She could never go home again.

It had hit her suddenly, a cruel blow battering her in her exhausted state. That she was totally cut off from her past, rootless in a present she hadn't chosen for herself. The numb acceptance of months had shattered, leaving her raw and scared and alone.

She had tried to see a future for herself, and had found only walls and aloneness.

Lara didn't know what she would have done if she hadn't seen the advertisement in the newspaper. Her only thought as she'd read the notice of auditions at the community theater had been to go, to escape the enclosing walls of her apartment.

So here she was. There were people around her who were brisk and friendly, who accepted what she seemed to be with utter unconcern. There was life around her, the chaos of creativity, the thudding pulse of activity. And it had helped her. She had felt herself steadying, calming, rediscovering her lost balance.

"Good night, Lara."

"Good night. See you tomorrow."

She responded automatically to the farewells, rolling the script up in one hand and using the other to fish in the pocket of her jeans for her car keys as she left the now deserted stage and headed up the dim aisle toward the front of the building. She had parked out front, learning later that everyone left their cars behind the theater. Absently, she made a mental note to park around back tomorrow night.

The lobby was silent, the dim light throwing eerie shadows into the corners. Lara walked a bit faster, conscious of those walls leaning in at her; she felt relieved when she pushed open one of 'the heavy doors and stepped out onto the sidewalk.

Pinewood was a small town, and like all small towns, it closed early. The theater was on Main Street, where, now, three traffic lights blinked an idle yellow caution above deserted blacktop. Shop windows glowed faintly from single lights left on to discourage theft, and old-fashioned parking meters dotted the curbs like lonely sentinels.

Lara's small car was parked across the street by one such meter, which she'd fed quarters into. Still, she half-expected to find a parking ticket fluttering on the windshield.

She was no more than three steps into the street when she heard the screech of tires. From the north end of town, a battered pickup truck suddenly careened around a corner and roared toward her, fishtailing wildly.

Blinded by the headlights and pinned in their glare, Lara waited numbly like a rabbit staring at a diving hawk.

Two

Lara couldn't make a sound. She couldn't move or think. All she could do was stand frozen and stare at the vehicle bearing down on her. It couldn't have been more than twenty feet away when she was suddenly yanked back out of the street and held in powerful arms against a hard body.

Vaguely hearing the truck roar past, Lara didn't try to free herself. The man held her tight. His fingers bit into her arm, and she was absurdly conscious of the faint, musky scent of his after-shave or cologne. Her face was pressed into his shoulder, and the arms around her were so strong. . . .

Those powerful arms loosened suddenly, and one of his hands gently turned her face up. "Are you all right?"

His eyes were colorless pools in the faint light, his hard, handsome face still and unreadable. Lara drew a deep breath, too numb from the shock to feel much else. "Yes. Yes, I think so. It must have been a drunk driver." Her voice sounded normal, she thought. Too normal.

A frown drew his flying brows together. "What else could it have been?"

"Nothing else. Of course, nothing else." She was still holding her script and keys, and bemusedly looked down at her hands. "Thank you for pulling me out of the road. I couldn't move for some reason. Stupid."

"Natural," Devon Shane corrected, that haunting voice of his cool and calm. "You shouldn't drive yourself tonight; I'll take you home."

"You don't have to—"

He ignored the protest. "Will you need your car tomorrow?"

"No. But I can't leave it here."

Devon took the keys from her nerveless fingers. "I'll park it around back so you won't get a ticket. Wait here."

She half-turned to watch him stride across the street, but waited obediently on the sidewalk. Obedient. *Obedient.* Her mind began working again, and she felt a pang of self-disgust. When had that happened to her? When had the numbness of shock and grief become this apathetic willingness to do only what she was told, to wait for others to guide her?

She had never been that way—before. She had charged at life, taking responsibility for her own sometimes reckless actions and stubbornly resisting any guiding hand. But then all control over her life had been snatched away from her, leaving her rudderless and stunned, and she had been forced by the sheer madness of the situation to accept guidance.

That had been natural, she thought now, and reasonable; she couldn't have coped on her own, and she knew it. But somewhere in these last months, acceptance had become a kind of mindless docility, and that was wrong. Wrong.

Lara started slightly as a car drew up to the curb before her, but she didn't move as Devon got out and came around to open the passenger door for her.

"Get in," he said.

She found herself taking a step toward him, then stopped jerkily. Who was he, after all? A stranger. Just a stranger with a haunting voice and burdened eyes. Just a man she didn't know, a man she couldn't trust.

"Lara." He held out one hand to her. "Come on."

She couldn't see his face clearly, and his curiously moving eyes were only dark pools, but his voice . . . his haunting voice. She saw her hand reach out slowly until his long fingers closed around it, and his strong, warm touch was like a lifeline.

Seconds later, waiting for him to move around to the driver's side after he closed her door, Lara thought vaguely, *She would have let down her braid, Nick. Without looking. Without even hesitating. Any woman would.*

"Where do you live?" Devon asked, sliding into the car beside her.

"About two miles away." Her voice was steady. "On the main road. Just head south."

He put the car in gear, but didn't release the brake. "Do you want to report it to the police?"

"No. I couldn't identify the truck. Unless you—?"

Devon turned the wheel and pulled the car away

from the curb, heading south. "It happened too fast," he said. "I didn't see enough to make an identification either."

There was silence for a few moments, and Lara was so aware of the man beside her that she could hardly think. What on earth was wrong with her? "I—I've never seen you around here." Not that she got out much, but, still, it was a small town. And she would definitely have noticed him.

"I've been here only a few days," he said. "I was transferred from the West Coast."

She glanced at him. "Oh? What do you do?"

"I work at Com-Tech. Do you know it? The big plant on the other end of town."

Lara nodded. "It's an electronics plant."

"Right. I work in conceptual design." He sent her a brief look. "How about you?"

"I work in design too. A different kind. I'm a commercial artist, an illustrator."

"Freelance?"

"Yes. I work out of my apartment." She hesitated, then said, "It was an impulse, auditioning for the play. I've never done any acting before. Have you?"

"In college. It's a good way to meet people when you're new in town."

New in town. She wondered if the driver of that truck had been new in town. Until now, the lingering shock and Devon's effect on her senses had kept her from thinking about the near miss, but she couldn't block it out any longer. She could feel inner tremors building, the numbness of shock giving way to the first icy prickles of fear. A drunken driver? Or something else, something that hadn't been random, hadn't been accidental?

Had Devon saved her from an accident—or a murder attempt?

"Lara?"

She clenched her teeth to prevent them from chattering. "It's just up ahead," she muttered. "The apartment building on the left." She could feel the glance he sent her, but he said nothing as he guided the car into the parking lot beside the big, five-story building.

"My keys—" she began, but Devon was turning off the engine, getting out of the car. She waited until he opened her door, then got out herself and said, "Thank you for—for everything."

"I'm coming up with you," he said briefly, shutting the car door and taking her arm.

"You don't have to." The forced calm in her voice was deserting her, leaving a wavering sound behind it.

"I know that." His fingers tightened gently around her arm. His free hand pushed open the entrance door for them, and he frowned slightly as he guided her inside. "Which floor, Lara?"

"Third. Apartment 304." She answered automatically, wondering in bewilderment what it was about his deep voice that tugged at her so.

There was no elevator. They went up the carpeted steps of the central, well-lighted stairwell in a silence broken only by the occasional faint sounds of music or television from inside the apartments they passed. When they reached her door, Devon produced her keys and unerringly selected the correct one.

Lara had left the living room lamps on. She always left a light on, even during the day, reluctant to take the chance of returning to darkness. Her apartment was decorated in soft pastels, the furniture was comfortable. And yet, it was an impersonal place, lacking a sense of its occupant. The framed prints on the walls were the kind that could have been found in any hotel room, and the color scheme blended with the bland touch of professional decorating.

Only the drafting table set up in one corner near a window struck a somewhat personal note, with drawings still pinned to it, and a clutter of supplies beside it.

Devon glanced briefly around the room, then guided her to sit at one end of the couch. He dropped her keys on the glass-topped coffee table. "Where's your kitchen?"

She nodded toward the short hallway leading off the living room, not trusting herself to speak. She didn't look at him as he left the room, just remained where he'd placed her with her fingers tightly laced together in her lap. A very quiet and sane voice in her head told her that she had every right to feel frightened, that it was a bit too coincidental that an anonymous driver had so narrowly missed her tonight.

But it just didn't make sense, she argued with the voice. It didn't. It was such a chancy thing, hit and run, with so many possibilities of failure. Guns, a bomb, that made sense; she would have expected something like that. In fact, had expected it.

Lara felt her lips twist bitterly. But what did she know about it, after all? Books, television, the movies. She didn't even know enough to be sure there was a reason for her fear.

A distraction from her chaotic thoughts presented

itself as Ching crawled out from under the couch and leapt lightly up onto the coffee table. He was a strange cat. Technically he would be labeled a tabby-point Siamese. His thick coat was a pale shade between cream and gray, and the markings on his face, paws, and tail were faint blue-gray stripes. He wore a leather collar with a silver bell that never made a sound unless he wanted it to.

In the five years that Ching had condescended to live with her, Lara had heard more than one baffled attempt to describe him; none of them quite hit the mark. Not only was he oddly colored and unusually large at almost twenty-five pounds, none of it fat, but he was uncatlike in behavior and in language; no sound even resembling a "meow" had ever escaped him. Oh, Ching talked. He muttered, he grumbled, he commented, he even cooed to wary birds outside the apartment windows. He always sounded polite, except when he was being profane, and his pale, aqua-blue eyes were eerily human in their expressiveness.

Now, sitting on the coffee table so that his long, ringed tail hung over the edge and swung slowly like a pendulum, Ching glanced toward the hallway and then at Lara. There was a question in the look.

"Company," she murmured. She'd stopped feeling peculiar talking to her cat, deciding that anyone who lived with Ching would have talked to him. It was a compulsion. One just couldn't help it, somehow.

Ching half-closed his pale eyes and lifted his chin. "Yah," he said softly. He was smiling. Most cats, Lara had decided, wore an almost permanent smile because their faces were made that way. But not her cat. Ching smiled only when he wanted to. And, despite his Oriental antecedents, his pointed face was wholly scrutable. Right now, he was pleased. Lara eyed him uncertainly. What did he have to be pleased about? Surely not Devon's presence. Ching's habit of hiding under furniture whenever there were visitors had been born in kittenhood; a gregarious cat when he was taken outside his own domain, he tended to be suspicious of invaders and disliked being visited himself.

Before she could react to the unusual pleasure of her cat, Devon returned to the living room and sat down on the couch beside her. He was holding two cups and handed one to her.

"Tea?" she asked, accepting the cup.

"Hot and sweet. Drink it, Lara."

She sipped cautiously, unwilling to look at him; they weren't in the dark any longer, and she felt wary of seeing that strangely moving pain shadowing his eyes. Forcing her voice to remain even, she said, "The traditional remedy for shock. Do you think I'm in shock?"

"I'd be surprised if you weren't. You could have been killed a little while ago."

"I—I would have been, if you hadn't—"

"My pleasure," he interrupted.

Lara frowned at her tea. "What were you doing out front, by the way? Your car was parked in back."

"Nick asked me to check the front door and make certain it was locked."

Perfectly reasonable, of course. Lara told herself not to be so damned suspicious. Devon certainly hadn't been driving that truck. She looked at Ching, finding his gaze fixed meditatively on Devon. Unable to help herself, she stole a glance at the man, and saw that he was returning the cat's steady regard.

"Ching, I gather?" he murmured.

"Yes."

"Hello, Ching." Devon's voice was conversational.

"Prroopp," the cat responded politely. His smile widened, curling up at each end. Suddenly, he reminded Lara of the Grinch, evilly bent on stealing Christmas—or whatever else wasn't nailed down.

She took a hasty sip of her tea, stole another glance at Devon, and found herself caught. He was looking at her, and with only a foot or so separating them, his eyes were far too intense. She felt a pang she couldn't define, a strange tug inside her, as if he held one end of a link that was connected to some vital part of herself.

"Was it just an accident, Lara?" he asked softly.

His voice wasn't fair. It wasn't fair. "What else could it have been?" she managed to ask unsteadily.

"You tell me."

"It was probably a drunk driver."

"Was it?" His lean face, so expressionless until then, changed, softened somehow as a faint smile curved his lips. It wasn't a humorous smile, and yet it held a curious charm. "Then why are you afraid?"

"I'm shaken up. You said it yourself—I'm in shock." She had gained control of herself by then, refusing to give in to panic or fear or him.

"And I'm a stranger," he said.

"Now that you mention it, yes." She lifted her chin much as Ching had done, but she wasn't smiling.

What might have been a glint of amusement stirred in his eyes. "In some cultures, saving a life means it belongs to you afterward."

"Not in this one."

"Yes. Pity."

Lara felt a little puzzled, and very wary. She had seen purely male interest in a man's eyes before, and was startled to recognize it in Devon's. Her own reaction to such interest in the past had been somewhat tepid, leaving her with the conclusion that she wasn't a sensual woman. But that unsettling warmth in Devon's eyes awoke something she'd never felt before, something that made her ache. She remembered the stark feeling of his hard, powerful body against hers, and heat curled in the pit of her belly.

She jerked her gaze from him, staring down at her cup. Dangerous. Lord, how dangerous it was for her to feel this for a stranger.

"Lara?" He watched her, aware that she was shaken not only by the near miss, but by him as well. He had felt it himself, that strange, instant affinity; he didn't like it, and he didn't trust it. He was tired, she was vulnerable. It was just that. Only that.

But he couldn't stop looking at her, couldn't block this intense awareness of her. Not what he had expected. What had he expected? A shattered woman, perhaps? She certainly wasn't shattered. Her pale green eyes, a shade as bright as new grass, held no defeat; she was wary and controlled, but it was obvious the numbness was dissolving. Would she panic now that someone was bent on disrupting the stalemate of months? Somehow, he didn't think so. Panic, he thought, was alien to this woman's nature.

"Lara, look at me."

She did, her gaze steady and guarded. No, he thought, there was no panic. Shadows, yes. Pain. Loneliness that came of being set apart from others. But shrewd intelligence and humor and perception lurked in her eyes.

He told himself that he was a bastard; it wasn't the first time such a thought had occurred to him. He smiled. "Have dinner with me tomorrow night, after rehearsal?"

"I don't think—"

"Please?"

Lara found herself nodding, and she was hardly surprised by her acceptance. That dark velvet voice . . . She got up when he did, waiting while he took his cup to the kitchen.

"Housebroken," he offered with a smile when he came back into the living room.

"Only because you want to be," she said involuntarily.

He chuckled, but didn't comment. Instead, he said, "Since your car's back at the theater, I'll pick you and Ching up tomorrow for rehearsal. We can bring him back here before we go to dinner. Quarter to six?"

"Fine," she murmured, wondering if she was out of her mind. Almost certain that she was.

"See you then." And he was gone.

Lara locked the door after him, then went back into the living room and stared at her cat. "You were a lot of help," she told him with a shaky little laugh.

Ching sat on the coffee table exactly as he had the entire time Devon had been there. His long tail waved slowly below him; his chin was up, his eyes were half-closed, and there was a distinctly unfeline smile on his pointed face. "Yah," he said softly.

"You're weird. You're a weird cat."

He blinked seraphically and began to purr. Ching's purr was no more feline than his other sounds, since it resembled a cross between a human's tuneful hum and the flutter of a bird's wings. It was also extremely loud. Lara had gotten used to it, but it tended to unnerve others—particularly since the hum held a definite but elusive tune, always the same one, that no one had yet been able to identify. A veterinarian had once confided to her that a cat's purr was one of the mysteries of science; he wanted to do a paper on Ching.

Lara moved about the apartment getting ready for bed. She kept her mind blank, unwilling to think about the confusing day behind her or the potentially troubling ones ahead. Still, she was conscious that whatever happened, the limbo of these past months was ended.

She wasn't sure how she felt about it. Emotions couldn't exist in a limbo. No pain or fear, no grief. It provided a kind of peace, even if that was only an illusion.

Sometimes, she thought, illusions were better than reality. Sometimes, illusions were the only havens left.

Out of habit, she turned off her bedside lamp before moving across the dark room to open the drapes. Also because of habit, she looked out first. Since her apartment windows faced front on the main street of town, it was well lighted outside. Across the deserted street was another group of apartments, this one set at right angles; the sidewalk there was in shadow. A faint motion caught Lara's attention, and she stood perfectly still, her eyes straining.

At the corner of the apartment building directly across the way, a patch of darkness moved slightly. Lara waited, holding her breath unconsciously. She stood there for a good five minutes, but couldn't be sure if she had seen someone leave. Or arrive. Or if she had seen anyone at all. Was someone watching her building? Perhaps even this window?

She left the drapes closed and crawled into bed feeling distinctly uneasy. Ching was already stretched out under the covers. She stroked his warm flank and listened to his rasping purr, and stared at the dark ceiling.

At one end of town near a shadowed street corner, a call was placed from an unlighted phone booth. The caller, insubstantial in the dimness, waited for a response, and then offered a flat statement as greeting.

"It's started."

The voice on the other end was impersonal. "Does she know?"

"She's no fool. What do you think?"

"You'll have to move fast then."

"Yes."

"Backup?"

"No. Not yet."

"It's your call." The voice was accepting. "Keep in touch."

"Right." The caller hung up, then glided away from the dark booth like a shadow.

On the opposite end of town, another call was placed, this one from a lighted booth at a convenience store. As before, the conversation was terse and largely without emotion.

"Are you in?"

"Yes. She's taking part in a community theater production. So am I."

"Anything yet?"

"I threw a scare into her tonight. I have a few more planned. We'll see."

"Search her apartment."

"Of course."

"We have to have those documents."

"I know. If she has them, I'll find them. If she doesn't have them—"

"Kill her."

There was a pause, and then the caller said slowly, "That wasn't the deal, unless she proved to be a threat."

"It is our new understanding," the voice said with forced patience, "that she could conceivably know more than we realized. Even without the documents, she's a threat. Make certain about the documents first—then kill her."

"Another thousand."

"You'll get it. When she's dead."

"Very well."

"Keep in touch."

"Right." The caller hung up, then strolled away from the convenience store, whistling softly.

When Devon arrived at Lara's apartment the following evening, she was waiting with a calm she had wrestled into place. After lying awake half the night, she had abruptly fallen into a deep sleep, from which only Ching's insistent demands for breakfast had roused her. She had managed to work a couple of hours during the day, and had thought a great deal.

The result was her state of calm, and it was different from that of the last months. She wasn't sure how exactly, but it wasn't a limbo, and even though some part of her longed to feel that mindless peace again, she was ready to begin living once more.

"Hi," Devon greeted her casually as she opened the door to him.

"Hello."

He looked at the big cat in her arms. "Does he have a carrier? I don't know about cats being loose in cars."

"He has a carrier," Lara admitted, feeling Ching stiffen at the hated word. "But I wouldn't subject you to that."

"What do you mean?"

"Within half a block, there'd be a report to the police that you were torturing somebody in your car."

"Some*body*?"

"Trust me. Ching doesn't sound like a cat when he howls. And he would howl." She smiled a little at Devon's look of amused surprise. Odd, she thought, that her first impression of him had been one of an enigmatic lack of emotion; his lean, handsome face seemed very expressive to her now. "He's well trained," she added. "He'll behave."

"A trained cat," Devon murmured, stepping back so she could come out into the hall. "I always thought that was a contradiction in terms."

"With most cats, it is," she agreed, leaving her apartment and watching him firmly close the door. "Not with Ching."

A few moments later, Devon had to agree that Lara's cat was well trained. Ching sat on the seat between them, his head as high as Devon's shoulder, since he was sitting up. The cat obviously needed to see where they were going. His front paws dangled, and his pointed face was lively with interest.

"He looks like a rabbit," Devon said after a glance.

Ching mumbled something, but didn't look at the man.

"Did he just swear at me?" Devon asked, startled.

"Probably. He doesn't like rabbits. Ching, behave!"

Devon's lips twitched. "Why do I get the feeling he's going to steal every scene?"

Lara smiled ruefully. "He just might."

When they reached the theater, it became clear that Ching was going to steal the hearts of almost everyone involved in the production—whether or not he stole scenes from the actors. From the moment Lara carried her cat backstage, he was the center of attention.

Hardly an indiscriminate cat, Ching developed a different attitude toward each person. He beamed at Nick's wife, Susie, but was politely unresponsive to the director's attempts to charm him. He was somewhat suspicious of Tim, was affable with Pat and Sonia, and hissed at Melanie when she tried to pet him. He took an active dislike to two of the stage crew, including Luke, whose tickle beneath the cat's chin provoked a muttered comment from Ching that was so profane it easily crossed the boundaries of language.

"Cats usually like me," Luke said in surprise.

Ching, sitting on one end of the old wooden table, tilted his head to look up at the man through slitted eyes. "Yah!" he said with distinct animosity.

Luke took a step back, almost comically bewildered. "What'd I ever do to you, cat?"

"I'm sorry, Luke, Melanie," Lara said helplessly. "He just doesn't take to some people."

"But will he take to stage direction?" Nick asked, eyeing his newest actor with foreboding.

Lara nodded reassuringly. "He has a large vocabulary, Nick, and he enjoys participating. He'll be fine."

"A large vocabulary? Show me," Nick requested.

As always, and totally unlike most cats, Ching went through his paces flawlessly. He knew all the standard canine obedience commands—though Lara prudently made them requests—and in addition was familiar with an impressive number of commonly used words.

"How long will he stay in one place once you've told him to?" Nick asked.

"Until I call him."

"You're sure?"

"Unless something's about to fall on him, he'll stay put."

Susie, who had watched intently, sighed and said, "Lara, I wish you'd tell me your secret. My cat barely knows his name."

Lara smiled a little. "Sorry, it wasn't my doing, not really. Ching learned most of this on his own. I just happened to notice one day. He's a bit . . . unusual."

Ching began purring.

"I'll say," Nick muttered, staring at the cat. "There's a—that's a definite tune. Isn't it?"

"I think so," Lara admitted. "But I've never been able to identify it."

They all listened intently for a few moments while Ching purred and gazed at them beatifically.

"Beats me," Luke said finally, and hearing a call from one of his men on stage, he wandered away.

34

Lara glanced at Devon, who had taken a chair at the table and was frowning slightly as he looked at Ching. The frown gave his handsome face a hard look of danger, and she felt unsettled by it. Then he seemed to feel her gaze, and the frown vanished as he looked at her and smiled.

The smile unsettled her even more.

"I can't get the tune," Nick said with a shrug. "Maybe one of us'll get it eventually. In the meantime let's run through the rest of the script, and then Susie wants to measure you for costumes. Sonia, Pat, you two go ahead, since you aren't in this act."

Ching remained where he was on the end of the table, seemingly paying close attention as the remaining actors went over their lines with Nick. He continued to purr until the director spoke firmly to him.

"Ching, we can't hear ourselves over your music."

The cat studied him for a moment, then stopped purring and began washing a striped forepaw.

"Damn," Nick muttered, then cleared his throat. "Fine. Okay—um—Lara, it's your line."

The reading continued without incident. They finished with this first run-through less than an hour later. Susie commandeered Devon for measurements and took him back to the dressing rooms, and Lara wandered out on stage. She'd left Ching to be petted and talked to by Sonia and Pat while a wary Melanie watched and Nick frowned over the notes on his script.

"How'd it go?" Luke asked cheerily, approaching where she stood near the wings.

"Fine, I guess." Lara slid her hands into the pockets of her denim skirt and shrugged. "I've never been in a play before, so I'm not really sure. The stage is looking good." She studied the garden scene, where the witch was to make her evil bargain with Rapunzel's father.

"I'm waiting for Nick's approval," Luke confessed. "I've never been involved with a play either."

"You haven't?" She looked up at him. "I thought community theaters would use the same stage crews every time. I don't know why I assumed that, but—"

"They usually do, I understand," Luke agreed. "But Nick's foreman was out of town or something, and he advertised. I happened to be passing through town—I'm sort of a gypsy at the moment—and I answered the ad. Which is why I'm here losing my heart to Rapunzel."

"Blarney," she scoffed, accepting his words as lightly as they were uttered.

Luke assumed a hurt expression. "Now, is that any way to treat a man who lays his heart at your feet? Of course, I realize that I'll have to win over Ching first, but I have plans."

"Good luck."

He eyed her. "You don't think I can do it?"

"I imagine you could," she said politely. "And I imagine the sun could rise in the west, given a slight change in the earth's orbit."

Luke winced, but rallied quickly. "Tomorrow, I'll come armed with tuna. In the meantime, have dinner with me tonight."

She smiled. "Sorry. I have plans."

"Tomorrow night then?"

"Why don't we wait until tomorrow?"

He sighed heavily. "I know what it is. Somebody

else got here before me, damn him. No ring, so it can't be a husband. Fiancé? Boyfriend? Just tell me the scoundrel's name, and I'll beat him to a pulp."

"I don't approve of violence," she said, still casual.

"Lara, Susie's ready for you," Devon said, emerging from the shadows of the wings.

"Thanks." She smiled apologetically at Luke, who shrugged cheerfully and went back to work. She walked past Devon, giving him another smile, which he returned, then headed backstage toward the dressing rooms. Wondering suddenly how much Devon had heard of her conversation with Luke, she glanced back over her shoulder at him just before he was out of sight.

He was standing with his hands in his pockets, gazing across the stage toward Luke. He wasn't smiling any longer. His handsome face was still and hard.

And dangerous.

Three

Lara told herself that her own uneasiness was making her suspicious of everything, but it didn't help much. That look on Devon's face bothered her; it hadn't been jealousy or dislike of another man's attentions to her, of that she was sure. It had been something else, something she couldn't define.

She stood in the dressing room while Susie measured her, then draped fabric around her, barely aware of the other woman's occasional enthusiastic comments. She kept remembering her first impression of Devon as enigmatic and dispassionate, and reminded herself that he could well be a natural actor with the ability to cloak his true nature. But what was his true nature? *Was* he as complex as she was beginning to believe? Were his motives for the apparent interest in her as straightforward as they seemed?

He had listened to her conversation with Luke; she was sure of it. But what did it mean? That hard stare at Luke . . . Not jealousy or possessiveness, but—what?

Was she imagining things?

Almost an hour later, as she sat across from Devon in a booth in one of Pinewood's few restaurants, she still wasn't sure. Devon was smiling at her, but not even the easy charm he could apparently turn as if with a switch could hide the shadows in his eyes; and his burdened look tugged at her, virtually making her forget her vague suspicions.

"You're very quiet," he said. "Is it because Ching was upset with us for abandoning him at your apartment?"

"No." She smiled. "He knows just how to make me feel guilty, but I've gotten used to it."

"Then what is it?"

Lara realized she was pushing the food around on her plate and eating very little. "I'm not very hungry, that's all."

"Sure it's not the company?" he asked lightly.

"No, of course not."

"Polite. But is it the truth?"

"Why would I lie?"

"Never answer a question with another question."

She managed a laugh. "Sorry. I wouldn't be here with you if I didn't want to be. How's that?"

"Better." His smile faded slightly. "But I'd be happier if you could bring yourself to say my name."

She looked at him, startled.

"You haven't, you know."

"I'm sorry, Devon."

"I hope it gets easier with practice. Especially since we're supposed to be lovers. Eventually."

Lara had the strong feeling that he wasn't talking

about the play. But before she could comment he was going on in the same easy tone.

"Nick did a good job adapting the fairy tale, don't you think? I read the original version last night; it's strictly a bare-bones kind of story."

"Most fairy tales are," she said, matching his tone. "Just moralistic fables for children."

"Nick's story isn't for children. How do you feel about that, Lara?"

The sudden change from the general to the specific caught her off guard, and she couldn't look away from his intense eyes. She cleared her throat with a husky little sound. "As you said, Nick did a good job of adapting it for the stage."

"And for adults." His smile went a bit crooked. "Lots of passionate embraces in his version. Before we begin rehearsing on stage, I thought we should talk about that."

"Oh?" She managed to yank her gaze from his, looking around the almost-deserted restaurant with what she hoped was careless interest. "I don't see why."

"Lara."

That haunting voice. Tugged at irresistibly, she found herself meeting his gaze again. She'd never been so conscious of her name as when he spoke it, and she had never been so aware of her body as when he looked at her. "Stop it," she whispered, not even sure what she was demanding.

His face seemed to harden slightly as he looked at her, as though everything inside him went still for an instant. His eyes darkened, something hot and primitive flashing in their shadowy depths. "No. I can't stop it. And neither can you."

Lara felt a stab of stark excitement, so piercing it stole her breath. He might as well have spoken a rawly sexual invitation, one her body responded to like kindling to a match. It was there, in his voice, something so utterly male it held the ancient sounds of battle and struggle and mating, as if it came from the caves.

Dear God . . . He wasn't touching her; there was a table between them. He was totally still, yet she felt enclosed by him. Her heart was hammering, and every nerve in her body felt as if it lay exposed and quivering, as if he had stripped her naked and left her achingly vulnerable. She had never in her life felt desire for a man, and she now had a single, awed thought: *If he can do this to me with just his voice . . .*

She should have been frightened. It was too soon for them and too new to her for this to be something she could possibly understand or accept. But that peculiar link between them, the tugging inside her, left no room for fear. There was only want, filling her until she ached with it.

Devon swore roughly beneath his breath and slid from the booth. Lara automatically matched his movements, vaguely aware that he had dropped money on the table, vividly aware of his big hand grasping hers in a strong, warm hold as he led her from the restaurant. She felt dazed, shocked by her response but not willing to fight it.

There was enough light in the parking lot for her to see his face as he stopped beside his car and turned to her. She had the sudden realization that he was angry, and that perception was borne out when he released her hand and lifted both of his hands to frame her face. His hands were hard, yet his touch was gentle.

"This wasn't supposed to happen," he said in a low voice that grated. "Dammit, Lara—"

She wasn't afraid of him. She thought dimly that perhaps she should be afraid of him, because the anger in him was dark and powerful and violent. But he wasn't angry with her, she knew that somehow, and it was enough. Staring up into the dark pools of his eyes, she managed a shaky smile. "I—I didn't expect it either."

He was very still, gazing down at her. She could almost feel a struggle going on in him, a terrible silent battle, and she was suddenly afraid that she would be on the losing side. She didn't want to lose, even though she couldn't have defined what her loss would have been; she knew only that she needed something in him and didn't care what it might cost her.

Her hands lifted to his chest, fingers probing compulsively to seek hard muscle beneath the bulky wool of his sweater. "Maybe I'd better ask if—if you're involved with somebody," she murmured. His broad chest moved as he sighed roughly.

"I am. I'm involved with you." The words were terse, almost reluctant, but his deep voice was husky.

Some part of Lara's mind told her that this was insanity, that she had no right to get involved with any man, much less this virtual stranger. But he made her feel so alive, and she wanted to go on feeling that way.

"Devon—" She had no idea what she was going to say, but whatever it was she never got the chance to say it. His powerful arms closed about her, pulling her fully against his hard body, and his mouth captured hers.

Captured like something he thought might escape him.

He didn't waste time with the slow, tentative explorations of a first kiss; there was no hesitation in him, no supplication. With a certainty she couldn't begin to fight, he demanded—and took—what belonged to him.

Lara had never been kissed like that before. His lips were passionate, insistent, holding a stark need that seared her to her bones. The sensations and emotions rushing through her body and mind were so wild she almost cried out with the force of them. Her mouth opened willingly to his, her arms going around his lean waist and holding on to him.

She didn't give a damn that they were standing in a parking lot in full view of anyone who happened to look, and she didn't feel the faint chill of the fall night. All she could feel was the heat blooming inside her and the hard strength of his body. And she could only stare up at him dazedly when he finally lifted his head.

Devon drew a deep breath and muttered an oath. He set her away from him firmly, then opened the car door and put her into the passenger seat without another word. Lara said nothing, at first because she wasn't sure she could speak and later because she didn't know what to say. So the drive to her apartment was a silent one.

Lara honestly didn't know what would happen once they reached her place. Despite his unhidden hunger, she thought that Devon was still struggling against something, still fighting not to give in to his own passion. It puzzled her. Did he expect her to demand some kind of commitment, was that it? Or was the burdened look in his eyes an indication of past hurts?

She didn't know how to ask him.

It was Devon who spoke first, taking her arm as they went up the stairs to her apartment. And though there was no evidence of strain on his hard face, the sound of it was in his voice.

"Tell me you don't want this, Lara."

They were at her door. She watched as he took her keys and unlocked the door, then looked up at him. His words had been a request rather than a challenge; he wasn't asking her to deny the desire between them, if she could, but to refuse to do anything about that desire.

She felt bewildered, half angry, and both emotions were reflected in her voice. "We aren't in high school, Devon," she said, keeping the words low because they were still standing before her unopened apartment door. "And I won't accept the sole responsibility of saying no. But I don't have to, do I? You've already said it."

"Lara—"

She snatched her keys from his hand and pushed open her apartment door, stepping inside and half-turning to shut him out.

"Yarrr!"

Lara had heard such a note in her cat's voice only once before, and the memory of that night would haunt her for the rest of her life. She went motionless, one hand on the doorknob and the other holding her keys and gripping the jamb with whitened fingers. She didn't have to look for Ching; he'd be under the couch.

Devon's hand covered the one on the jamb. "Lara? What is it? What's wrong?"

"Someone's been here," she whispered. "In the apartment."

Swiftly, he pushed the door farther open and stepped inside. In a low voice, he said, "Stay here, and don't close the door."

She didn't move, just leaned back against the jamb and watched as he went silently down the short hallway that led to the kitchen and bedroom. She knew she should go to the telephone and call the number she'd memorized. Anything suspicious, they'd told her, anything at all. They'd check it out, and if it proved to be a threat to her safety, she'd be protected.

Moved again. Uprooted, vanishing from this life only to appear in another one. Like a penciled line disappearing under the stroke of an eraser, Lara Callahan would simply cease to be.

No . . . not again.

Ching muttered softly from under the couch, and Lara closed the door and came into the living room. There was no one here now, she knew. She dropped her keys on the coffee table and gazed around the room for a moment, then crossed to her drafting board and stared at it.

"Nothing," Devon said, emerging from the hallway. "What makes you think someone was here?"

"Ching told me," she murmured.

"Where is he?"

"Under the couch."

There was a moment of silence, and then Devon

called the cat's name firmly. Lara half-turned to watch her feline friend emerge from beneath the couch and leap lightly to the coffee table, where he sat with flattened ears and a lashing tail.

"Yah!" he said in an emphatic tone.

Devon studied the cat, then looked at Lara. "He's obviously upset, but he was when we left."

Lara reached to unpin a drawing from the board, holding up the two pieces so that Devon could see them; a dreamy watercolor of a castle had been cut from corner to corner. "Just something I was doing for myself," she said in the same even, detached tone. She put the ruined picture down and added, "The knife cut right into the board."

"Are you going to call the police?"

"No. Nothing's missing. There won't be any finger-prints."

Devon took a step toward her, and his voice was taut when he demanded, "Lara, what the hell is going on?"

She went over to the couch and sat down, sud-denly aware of trembling legs. "What makes you think I know?"

"Don't give me that. I want an answer."

An answer, she thought. Well, she had her answer now. This wasn't a vague suspicion. This was fact. Someone had broken in to her apartment, had searched neatly and professionally through her be-longings, touched her clothing. She felt violated. And frightened. And alone.

"Lara." His haunting voice was quiet now. "Let me help you."

She couldn't trust him. She couldn't trust anyone—and how stupid of her to have forgotten that. "You're confusing the play with reality, Devon." Her voice sounded calm, she thought. "In real life, the prince never comes storming to the rescue."

He moved around the end of the couch and sat down beside her, not quite touching. "Give me a chance."

She didn't look at him; she didn't dare, wary of losing her precarious control. "I don't want this," she said clearly, giving him an answer he had demanded earlier. "You said you couldn't stop it. You said I couldn't, even though you wanted me to. But I will. I'll stop it. I don't want you in my life, Devon."

"You're lying," he said flatly.

Lara could feel the tension growing inside her, quivering like glass about to shatter. With all the will she could command, she kept her voice even and detached. "No. But it doesn't matter, does it? You wanted me to say no, and that's what I'm saying. Now, please leave."

"Look at me, Lara." When she didn't move, he leaned over and grasped both her shoulders, turning her firmly.

She wanted to flinch away from his touch, his gaze, because she knew her will could never stand against his. Not when he looked at her. Not when he touched her.

"Stop it," she whispered, just as she had in the restaurant. She was caught again, tugged at in that profound, overpowering way, and she couldn't fight it.

"I won't leave," he said. "I won't walk out because you're determined to face this, whatever it is, alone. I want you, Lara. And you want me. Admit it."

She had no choice. Even now, with the shadows

of fear closing in on her, she couldn't deny the effect he had on her. She wanted to throw herself into his arms, to be enclosed by him and revel in his warmth and strength.

"Yes," she admitted finally, defeated. "But you said—"

"Never mind what I said." A muscle tightened in his jaw. "Even if you'd told me you didn't want this, I probably—" He broke off, shaking his head. "Just never mind. We'll talk about all of it later."

Lara remained half-turned toward him as he released her and sat back. She knew what he wanted to talk about now, but she was still uncertain. Tell no one, they'd said. And she didn't know him, after all, no matter how he could make her feel. But he'd been with her; he couldn't be involved in it.

Could he? An accomplice could have done the dirty work while Devon charmed his way into her life . . . her bed.

"Don't look at me like that," he said in a sudden, low growling tone of voice.

She shifted her gaze to the hands clasped together in her lap, then looked back at him because she couldn't help herself.

He sighed roughly and half-lifted a hand as if to touch her. But the powerful hand fell back to his thigh and clenched briefly into a fist. "The truck last night," he said tersely. "Now your apartment. What's going on, Lara?"

Those burdened eyes. What would he do, she wondered dimly, if she offered him her own burden? Would his desire for her force him to share it? Or would her troubles quite effectively provide the no he had wanted her to utter?

"Dammit, Lara, tell me."

She felt a sigh escape her, but tried to warn him. "In real life, there are worse things than witches with spells . . . and prisons aren't always made of stone."

He looked at her for a moment, then asked quietly, "Are you imprisoned?"

"In a way."

"Tell me."

Was he involved? She didn't know, couldn't know. She gave him her trust blindly. And there was a certain relief in finally telling someone.

"A year ago I was living with my father in another state. He was working for an electronics company, where they designed state-of-the-art computers. The company held several government contracts, so everyone was upset, very upset, when it was discovered that some of their designs had been pirated."

"Industrial spies," Devon said. "It's been known to happen."

Lara remembered only then that he worked for an electronics company himself. "Yes. And if it had been only that, it would have been bad enough. But my father and others were working on several top secret projects, and when one of those designs came up missing, there was a general panic."

Devon waited for a moment when she fell silent, then prompted, "And so?"

She took a breath. "Security was tightened, and the government sent in investigators to try to find out who was responsible. My father was heading one of the research groups, so he worked closely with the investigators. They found nothing. The general belief was that someone on the inside had been selling the designs, but they couldn't discover who it was."

"Did your father agree with the general belief?"

"No. He didn't think someone on the inside had been seduced; he believed that one of his own people had been working for someone outside the company."

"Did he know who it was?"

"He suspected. Then, a few weeks later, he found something." Lara shook her head unconsciously. "I don't know how. I'm not even sure exactly what it was; the FBI talked about documents, but I never saw them. But Dad did tell me . . ."

"What?"

"That it was bigger than they'd suspected. That a . . . he called it a cartel of criminal businessmen had developed a system of planting spies into the most top secret high-tech government installations in the country."

"He was sure of that? He had proof?" Devon's face was intent, his eyes fixed on hers.

"He said so. He said he'd found the link, that he knew who the plant was inside his company, and that he'd learned the names of several people in other companies. I wanted to call the FBI right then, but he said he wanted to give them the whole package. That's the way he phrased it, 'the whole package.' I'd never seen him so upset, furious, and, I think, afraid."

After a moment, Devon asked, "What did he do?"

"He went out several times during the next week, and came back late. He spent hours locked in his study, working at his computer. He wouldn't tell me anything, just that he was tying all the loose ends together." She stopped, not sure she could tell Devon the rest of it.

He reached out and took one of her hands, holding it in a strong, warm grasp. "Tell me, honey."

The endearment startled her, and for the first time she understood why that word *was* an endearment. Like the substance it named, it was golden and unutterably sweet, with the cloaked wildness of something given by nature rather than man-made.

Her fingers twined unconsciously with his. "I don't think Dad suspected the cartel was on to him," she said unsteadily. "Otherwise, he would have sent me away. That night . . . I went out with some friends. When I came home, I didn't know there was anything wrong until I opened the front door. Ching howled, the way he did tonight."

"Yah," the cat murmured from his seat on the coffee table, apparently in response to his name.

Lara glanced at him blindly, then turned her unseeing gaze back to Devon. "Later, the FBI found out—I don't know how—that Dad had gotten some kind of warning. A phone call, maybe. They wouldn't tell me. But they were sure he'd had at least a few minutes to hide whatever evidence he had gotten together. They were sure of that."

Devon's fingers tightened gently around hers.

She hardly felt it. Her voice had become a monotone, each word dropped into place starkly. "I went across the hall and knocked on the study door. There wasn't an answer. The door wasn't locked. The room was a shambles, furniture overturned, books and papers scattered everywhere. Dad's safe was open—and empty.

"He was lying on the floor beside his desk. He was
. . . they'd beaten him."

Devon muttered something under his breath and
pulled her into his arms, holding her close against
him. Lara, cold and aching, accepted his comforting
and his warmth, realizing only then that no one had
ever held her to let her grieve for her father. She'd
had no other family, and the FBI had given her
friends no chance to contact her. She didn't cry,
because there were no tears left in her for the memory of that night, but she burrowed closer to Devon
with a shudder that shook her entire body.

"It's all right," he said softly after a few moments.
"It's all right, honey."

"No, it isn't." Her voice was thick, unsteady. "It'll
never be all right again." She pushed back away
from him, but didn't object when he kept one arm
around her shoulders.

Devon was a little pale, but his mouth curved in a
kind of wry self-mockery. "I'm sorry; I know platitudes don't ease the pain. No words could."

His burdened eyes told her he knew all about pain.
Drawing a deep breath, she said, "I called the FBI.
Dad was . . . there was nothing anyone could do for
him. Agents came. And they just took over. They
moved me to an apartment across town; they let me
pack a bag and take Ching, but nothing else. Later,
they talked to me, questioned me, for hours."

"About the documents?"

"Yes. They said that Dad had gotten a warning,
and that since the whole house had been searched
he must not have told those men where the evidence
was hidden. They thought I knew. But I didn't know."
She sighed raggedly. "They finally said that the car-

tel might believe I knew something, and that I was a target. So they put me in their protection program. Callahan isn't my real name; it's Mason. I get a new name, a new identity every time they move me in the protection program."

After a moment, Devon said quietly, "Imprisoned."

"I didn't realize at first," she murmured. "I was numb. I didn't care. It just hit me a few weeks ago. That I was cut off, rootless. And now . . ."

"Now, it looks like the cartel has found you. Is that it?"

"I don't know. Maybe."

"Maybe? Lara, you were nearly run down last night. Your apartment's been searched. What else could it be?"

"I just don't see the point," she told him, saying aloud what had been running through her mind. "The cartel has to know the FBI would be suspicious of any accident, so why try to run me down with a truck?"

"To scare you."

Lara grappled with that for a moment. "Because I might somehow lead them to the evidence against them?"

"They searched your apartment," he reminded her. "And they meant you to know it, because the only sign they left was that drawing cut in half."

She felt cold again. "Damn. Why can't everyone—the FBI, those criminals—realize that if I knew anything at all, I would have said so?"

"Maybe they think that you might know something you aren't consciously aware of," Devon suggested slowly.

"How could that be?"

He shook his head. "I'm not sure. Something you saw but didn't really notice; something you heard but didn't really listen to. I don't know."

"Neither do I. I've gone over it again and again in my mind. Do you think I could ever forget that night? Or the weeks before? I'll never forget, not any of it!"

Devon's arm tightened around her. "Easy," he murmured.

Lara took a steadying breath, then rose and began wandering restlessly around the room.

"You should call the FBI," he said.

"And be uprooted again? Lifted out of this cage and dropped into another one?" She laughed bitterly. "No, thanks. I won't run for the rest of my life."

"Then what?" His voice hardened. "Roll over and die for them?"

"They haven't hurt me."

"Not yet. Do you really believe they'll take the chance of leaving you alive when they think you know something?"

"I won't run. I won't."

"Lara, for God's sake, be reasonable."

She laughed again, not bitterly but not amused. "How ironic that I'm about to occupy center stage in a fairy tale. It isn't so easy to be a prince in real life, is it? Stay out of it, Devon. The witch might blind you for real. Or worse."

He rose from the couch, watching her as she paced the room. "You think I'm going to run out on you," he said slowly.

"I think you should," she said in a flat tone, not looking at him. "You'd be a fool not to. In real life, I don't need a prince—I need a bloody army." She was hardly aware of her own sardonic tone.

Devon chuckled suddenly.

Lara swung around to stare at him in surprise, then heard a giggle escape her. "Hysteria," she offered as an excuse for her choked laugh.

He was smiling a little. "No, just a sense of humor. But if you aren't willing to call out the FBI's army, I'm afraid you're going to have to settle for a prince. I'm not going anywhere, Lara."

"Now who's not being reasonable?" It was the only thing she could think to say.

He slid his hands into the pockets of his pants, powerful shoulders moving in a faint shrug. "I'll admit I've never thought of myself as a prince, but I'm willing to give it a shot."

"Why?"

His smile faded, then changed, reappearing as a sweet, determined expression that was indescribably male. "You know why."

Lara felt her knees weaken. The man possessed an uncanny ability to scatter what she fondly called her wits, she decided dazedly. She forced herself to make one last attempt to make him see this situation sanely. "Devon, *this* isn't a fairy tale; there won't be any helpful magic. It isn't a play; there won't be applause when it's over. It's real, and I can't see a happy ending."

"Maybe you're not looking hard enough."

"I don't dare look any harder." She had held her voice steady with great effort.

He came to her slowly, but didn't touch her when he stood only a foot or so away. There was an expression in his eyes she had seen before, that inward-turned anger that was so dark, and his handsome face tautened until it was almost masklike.

He's fighting again. The thought was clear in her mind, but the knowledge was bewildering. What was he fighting?

"Devon—"

"You can't talk me out of it, Lara." He was terse, his voice clipped. "So, we'd better come up with strategy of some kind."

"For instance?" She refused to admit to herself how relieved she felt. "Pull up the drawbridge and flood the moat?"

"I don't suppose you'd consider something along those lines?"

Lara shook her head. "No, not if you mean staying put in the apartment. Besides, this is hardly an impregnable castle, as the events of tonight proved."

He frowned. "They should have put you in a building with more security; the front entrance isn't even locked."

"This is a small town. Apartment buildings don't *have* security here. They've never needed it."

"*You* need it," he pointed out.

"Not now. I have a prince." She had intended to sound sardonic, but somehow her voice had emerged with a tremor in it.

Devon made a slight movement, as if he wanted to touch her. But he didn't. "Such as he is," he said lightly, then went on, "Look, it's late; we can talk about ways and means tomorrow. Why don't you go to bed. I'll bunk down on the couch—"

"No, you won't," she interrupted, controlling her voice this time and making it sound firm. "They won't try anything else tonight. If they'd wanted to, they would have been waiting here for me."

"Not if they knew I was with you."

"I'll be fine, Devon. Go home."

"Did anybody ever tell you that you're a stubborn woman?"

"Yes." She managed a smile.

He swore softly. "I don't want to leave you."

Lara chose to interpret that as concern about the possible danger rather than something more intimate. "I'll be fine," she repeated.

Devon stared at her for a moment, then bent and kissed her quickly. "If I didn't believe that," he said somewhat roughly, "I wouldn't be leaving. Lock the damned door."

She locked the door behind him, then leaned back against it for a moment. Oddly enough, there was little in her thoughts concerning faceless enemies trying to frighten her—or worse. She wandered back into the living room and looked at Ching, still sitting on the coffee table and regarding her enigmatically.

"How about that?" she murmured to him. "I have a prince."

"Yah," Ching said softly.

In his position across the street from the apartment building, the man was virtually hidden in the shadows. He watched the lighted windows on the third floor, his gaze shifting from time to time to probe the front entrance of the building. The rear entrance was barred from inside; he had checked.

The lights in the third-floor apartment went out, but the man didn't move. He barely noticed the increasing chill as the night wore on, and when muscles protested his stillness he flexed them absently and expertly without much movement; anyone passing by him in that moment would have seen nothing.

He watched, and the night passed. No one approached the apartment building across the street.

"Well?"
"She doesn't have them."
"You're sure?"
"Positive."
"Then—"
"We have another problem."
"What?"
"There's a joker in the deck."

Four

Lara worked most of the next day in her apartment. Devon called around nine, saying he'd just wanted to make sure she was all right. After saying he would pick her up at noon for lunch, he hung up somewhat abruptly. She wondered if he had guessed that, given half a chance, she would have avoided the lunch date.

The truth was Lara hardly knew what she was feeling—particularly about Devon. The sense of relief she felt in having shared her secret with him was almost overwhelming, and yet she was nagged by the awareness that she shouldn't have done it. She shouldn't have broken the most rigid rule of the federal protection program: Tell no one.

And even though her confession to him had brought relief, so much else hadn't been changed by it. She still felt isolated, alone. Separate.

And wary. Wary, especially, of Devon. He had said that he wouldn't leave, had seemingly accepted both her burdens and her unwillingness to call in the authorities; and yet, he was clearly struggling against his own desire for her.

"You've gone quiet on me again," he said.

He had surprised her by producing a picnic basket and then driving to Pinewood's single park, which was on the edge of town at a small lake. The fall day was clear and warm, the park virtually deserted, and they had spread their blanket near the lake.

Lara tried to think of a response to his remark, one he would accept. They had finished lunch, and had repacked the picnic basket. He was lying on his side, on one elbow, regarding her gravely. She thought he looked a little tired, as if he hadn't slept much.

"Lara?"

"You have the most amazing voice," she blurted.

One of his flying brows lifted, and the sapphire eyes held a flash of laughter before shadows replaced the amusement. "Have I?"

She looked at him somewhat helplessly. When he was with her, the suspicions faded away until they didn't seem to matter; it was when she was alone that those awful doubts crept in. "Yes. It—it just isn't *fair*, dammit!"

"Sorry," he murmured, smiling.

Lara fumbled for another topic. Without food to occupy their attention, she could no longer even try to block out her awareness of him. And, no matter what he'd said later, she couldn't help remembering that he had virtually told her to refuse him the night before.

"Don't you have to get back to your office?" she said finally. "It's after one."

"No, there's no hurry. Schedules are very informal in the design section. I think that's usually the case on the creative end of things."

"Unless—"

Devon's smile faded. "Unless it involves security clearances and the like. Is that what you're thinking?"

She shrugged, avoiding his intent gaze. "I guess."

He watched as she picked up a red autumn leaf from the ground beside the blanket and started twirling it between her fingers. "Is that why you've been so quiet? Because telling me about it last night brought back memories?"

Lara hesitated, then said, "What happened to my father was left unresolved, unfinished. His murderers were never identified, much less caught and tried, and the evidence he spent his last days working on was never found. It didn't have an ending. And until it does . . ."

"You won't be able to put it behind you," he said.

"No. That's why it's almost a relief to believe the cartel has tracked me down. *Something* is happening, and that's better than nothing. I wanted you to understand that."

He was silent for a moment, then said, 'I can understand that, Lara." His mouth tightened suddenly as he added, "But you're risking your life needlessly by refusing to contact the authorities."

"I told you. I don't want to be moved again, and that's what they'd do."

"I realize how you feel, but—"

"How can you?" She stared at him with burning eyes. "Have you ever had your roots cut away? Have you had to learn to answer to a strange name? Have you had to divide your life into two parts, and try to forget the first part ever existed?" She drew a shaky breath. "Every face could be an enemy, so you have to hide. You hate the fear, but you can't fight it, can't conquer it—not until there's an ending. And that ending could come tomorrow . . . or never."

"Lara . . ."

"It's like being half-alive," she whispered. "And all you can do is wait. In limbo. Like Rapunzel in her damned tower. I can't stand it anymore, Devon. I want my name back, and my life; I can't have either until it's over."

"I'm sorry," he said softly. He was very still.

She regained her control and made her voice even. "So am I. I shouldn't be dumping all this on you. But I haven't been able to talk to anyone about it."

Devon reached out suddenly and pulled her down beside him. He leaned over her, his wide shoulders blocking the sunlight. "I want you to tell me how you feel, honey," he said softly.

She gazed up into his shadowed eyes and knew he was lying. Her pain was a burden to him. She summoned a smile. "Never mind. I'll stop feeling sorry for myself. We should be getting back; you may not have a schedule, but I have a deadline and I need to work this afternoon." It was a lie, but Lara didn't care. Her whole life was a lie. Why balk at one more?

He stared down at her for an instant, something very like frustration tightening his handsome features. Then, with a curse muttered under his breath, he bent his head and kissed her fiercely, as if she were trying to elude him and he could keep her only with the power of his kiss.

Lara knew that she should fight her own response. This extremely complex man baffled her; she had the odd conviction that he was caught up in something beyond his control, just as she was, and that it was tearing him up inside. She was half-afraid to trust him, even though she had; and she tried to remember that some part of him was fighting this.

Yet she knew, with a certainty beyond question, that he *needed* this, just as she did. The inexplicable bond between them was something neither could fight, as if its roots were embedded too deeply inside them ever to be torn out except at the cost of mortal agony.

And her response came from that affinity, that shared, almost desperate need. She didn't understand it, but she could no more fight it than she could willfully stop breathing.

Her arms crept up around his neck, her fingers twining in the silky strands of his black hair. Her mouth came alive beneath the insistent pressure of his, opening to him. She felt one of his arms slip beneath the small of her back to press her firmly to his chest, while his other hand tangled in her hair. She heard a soft murmur of disappointment escape her lips when his mouth left them, but the dissatisfaction ebbed as he began exploring the sensitive flesh of her throat.

"Lara . . ." His voice was thick, impeded. "Lord, what are you doing to me?"

She caught her breath in a gasp as his lips settled over the pulse beating in her throat and she felt a jolt of exquisite pleasure. His touch evoked a sweet, stinging ache that spread throughout her body like ripples in a pool. She couldn't seem to breathe after that single gasp, as if even that life-giving function had suspended itself in taut waiting.

Then, suddenly, Devon released her, eased her hands away from him, and sat up. His shoulders were stiff, his face drawn. Without looking at her, he said, "Lara . . ."

Bewildered, she pushed herself up and sat staring at him. "What's wrong?"

In a low voice, he said, "When you believe there may not be a tomorrow, it's easy to follow your impulses. To give in to desires without dwelling on the consequences."

"Is that what you think I'm doing?"

Devon gave her an odd look, then sighed. "You have to be sure, that's all I'm saying."

She scrambled to her feet. "Fine. Ready to leave?"

He got up silently, gathering the blanket and basket and following her to his car. But instead of starting the engine immediately, he sat gazing through the windshield.

Lara couldn't help stealing glances at him, even though she felt cold and miserable. Part of her was angry that Devon was being rational about this, yet she was all too aware that he had been at least half-right, she couldn't deny her own reckless willingness to live right now, today. He made her forget everything when he held her in his arms, and she *wanted* that.

"Are we going?" she questioned abruptly, unable to bear the silence a moment longer.

He glanced at her, hesitated, then swore softly and started the car. When they reached her apartment building, he caught her wrist when she would have gotten hastily out of the car.

"Wait." He studied the front of the building almost absently, his gaze on a van with a landscaping service logo painted on it and two men energetically pruning bushes on either side of the front entrance.

Lara tried to pull away. "You don't have to come inside with me. I'll be fine, Devon."

He looked intently at her. "You've said that before."

"And I meant it." She kept her voice steady. "You were right. The last thing I need today is a fling. I'll wait and see if there's a tomorrow. Thanks for lunch."

"Your car's still at the theater," he said. "I'll pick you up at a quarter to six."

She pulled her hand away and got out of the car, closing the door without another word.

Devon watched her until she vanished inside the building. He returned his gaze to the gardeners at work, who had spared him no more than cursory glances. He put his hand on the gearshift, hesitated, then put the car in gear and drew away from the curb with a bleak sigh.

It was always difficult, he reminded himself savagely. But this time it was far worse than that. Lara wasn't an enemy. She was a lonely, wary woman trapped in a situation not of her making. She was so damned vulnerable, and he couldn't help but wonder if, like Rapunzel, she was bound to fall for the first man who found a way into her prison.

It was that as much as his own deception that was tearing him apart. Did she want him? Or would any "prince" evoke the same response in her? And if she wanted him, how would she feel when she discovered what he really was?

He longed to tell her, but couldn't. Her entire life was a lie, one she hated; what would she think of his lie? The thought wasn't really a question, because he knew what she'd think. He thought it himself.

"Bastard," he murmured.

"Lara, how about this?" Nick placed sheet music on the somewhat battered piano that stood center stage surrounded by the chaos of the stage crew.

She slipped onto the bench and studied the music, her pale and delicate face brightening as though someone had handed her a gift. "Beethoven's *Moonlight* Sonata," she murmured.

"You can play it?" Nick asked.

"Well, it's been a while," she said.

"Try."

From the shadows of the wings, Devon watched as the other actors gathered around the piano. Ching sat on top, motionless as a statue with his ringed tail neatly curled around his striped forepaws; like his human companions, his attention was focused on the woman who ran her long, agile fingers over the ivories experimentally.

Devon hadn't known what to say to Lara after their abrupt parting earlier in the day, and with her attitude of aloof courtesy, she hadn't offered an opportunity to say much of anything. She hadn't sulked or displayed either anger or resentment; she had simply withdrawn from him.

Devon hated that. He needed her so badly that he ached with it, but there was no way he could explain that to her—not without being forced to explain too many other things as well. God knew he wanted to explain it all, for his sake as well as hers, but he couldn't. Not yet.

Nor could he allow this taut distance between them to remain. It was dangerous, far too dangerous, for her to shut him out right now. She had to talk to him, had to confide her feelings and fears and memories. She had to. The answer was there, somewhere inside her, hidden because she couldn't bear to think about the night her father had been killed. And Devon had to have that answer.

He hadn't dared push her—yet. But he was intensely aware that time was running out. And he was left with the bitter knowledge that he would be destroying any possibility of a future between them if he pushed Lara, demanding her deepest trust while denying her *his* trust.

She wouldn't be able to forgive that.

Devon found that he was watching her as she coaxed resonant notes from the old piano, something in his chest hurting. She had said he had an amazing voice, and his amusement had been brief, quickly replaced by the knowledge that his voice was one of the reasons he was here. He himself heard nothing unusual in his voice, but had accepted the consensus that he could extract information where others failed.

It was his specialty.

Lara glanced up at Nick in surprise. "It's in tune." The piano looked, to put it mildly, as if it had been rescued from a condemned building.

"Yeah, I had it done this afternoon. Play."

"The entire sonata?" she asked with a smile.

"Sure. We'll pick out the passages we want later."

Lara nodded, and her expression became intent with concentration as she began playing the piece.

After the first haunting notes of the music rose

above the noise of the stage crew, Devon wasn't surprised to see the men gradually stop working on the exterior of a pseudostone tower and begin listening. Susie appeared from the opposite side of the stage with two costume sketches held in her hands and joined the group at the piano, her pretty face reflecting pleasure.

The music went on, a bit tentative in places because of Lara's lack of recent practice. Devon wondered idly what the group would say if he told them that Lara had won an international competition with this particular sonata less than ten years before.

He knew that. Just as he knew all the statistical facts of her life.

His gaze left the woman playing the piano and roved about the stage, automatically counting and arriving at the correct number; they were all here, and had been for nearly two hours. Nothing unusual had happened since he and Lara had arrived at the theater with Ching.

But she was in danger, dammit, and hell-bent against asking for any kind of help. After he had seemingly blown hot and then cold, she wasn't about to turn to him naturally; he would have to persuade her—and the thought of that left a bitter taste in his mouth.

He was going to be damned no matter what he did.

Devon made up his mind right then. It couldn't go on this way; he had to tell her. He'd see her safely home tonight, and then he'd call—

The thought ended with chilling abruptness. Her car. It had been parked behind the theater, right out in the open for anyone to see. For anyone to get at.

After making certain that the attention of everyone on stage remained focused on Lara, Devon eased farther back into the wings and then silently went backstage. He slipped out the back exit, closing the heavy fire door behind him with scarcely a sound. He went to his own car first, opening the trunk and removing several tools and a small device designed to receive and scan a number of electronic frequencies.

It was dark; there was only one security light behind the theater, and it was located a number of yards from the parked cars. Devon turned on his flashlight as he approached Lara's car, then spent some time on the ground examining the underside of the vehicle. He was quick, but thorough.

Nothing. The scanner remained mute, which indicated there was no device such as a bomb hidden in or under the car. But Devon knew that bombs weren't the only means of wrecking a car and occupant. He got to his feet and cautiously raised the hood, then bent and very carefully checked the engine, with his sensitive touch as well as the narrow beam of light.

No more than five minutes into his search, he found it. The steering mechanism had been tampered with. He remained perfectly still as he stared at the car. Lara would have left the theater with no idea that the two-mile drive back to her apartment would prove to be a game of Russian roulette; the sabotage was such that the steering might have failed at the first turn or the fifth. And even with the lower speed limit of the downtown area, there was every chance that she could have been seriously hurt.

Devon felt an icy rage grip him. They were playing cat and mouse with her, damn them, toying with her. First the near miss of the truck, then her apartment—and now this. They were trying to scare her, panic her. That was only the first step of their deadly little plan, he knew; the ultimate aim was to remove any threat Lara presented.

Time was running out.

He bent to the car again.

"You are terrific," Luke said with obvious sincerity.

Lara shrugged a little, but smiled at him. "Thank you. I'm afraid I'm out of practice, though."

They were standing by the piano; the others were some distance away, occupied with different tasks. Nick was critically examining the "stone" tower, Susie was talking to Melanie about her costume, and Tim was going over lines with the Arnolds. Devon was nowhere to be seen.

"You really are—" Luke began.

Ching interrupted with a muttered curse, staring at the man through slitted eyes.

Luke met that malevolent gaze, then looked back at Lara with a sigh. "The tuna didn't go over at all," he said mournfully.

"You tried?" Her tone was sympathetic.

"Yes, while you were trying on your wig backstage. He acted like I was offering him something unspeakable."

"I'm sorry, Luke. He's—he's really an odd cat."

Ching displayed every one of his pearly whites as he hissed softly, still glaring at Luke. His ears were beginning to flatten, while his ringed tail was puffing to twice its normal girth in an indication of feline rage.

"Behave!" Lara told him sharply.

The cat glanced at her, then grumbled something that was clearly profane. He turned his head pointedly away from Luke, removing himself spiritually from the entire situation.

Luke shrugged. "He hates me. I don't know why, but he hates me. My after-shave, d'you think?"

Before Lara could answer, the cat muttered again. She stared at him. "Ching." He looked at her, then leapt from the piano and stalked across the stage toward the wings. His angry noises grew louder with each step, finishing with an emphatic howl that momentarily halted every other sound on stage. Then he vanished into the shadows.

Lara smiled somewhat helplessly as several startled looks were directed toward her, then she looked back at Luke as the others resumed their activities.

"He isn't a cat," Luke said. "I don't know what he is, but he isn't a cat."

Her smile turned rueful. "I've often thought the same thing."

Luke sighed, then said, "Why don't we have dinner and discuss what he might be."

Remembering only then what they had talked about the evening before, Lara hesitated. Luke seemed as straightforward as Devon was complicated, and she wished the heart was a logical organ. But it wasn't. "Thanks, Luke, but I don't think so."

He eyed her for a moment in silence, then leaned back against the piano and folded his arms. "Devon?"

Luke's clear blue eyes were uncomfortably and unusually grave, and Lara found it impossible to lie outright. "Was that a question?" she asked lightly.

"Yes. But I'll spell it out if you like. Is Devon the reason you're turning me down?"

"Does it have to be another man?" she responded, thinking that the other man wouldn't let her get away with answering a question with another question.

"No. I think it is, though."

Lara shrugged. "We've seen each other a couple of times. Outside the theater, I mean."

Frowning a little, Luke said slowly, "I don't want to sound like a sore loser, but maybe you'd better be careful, Lara."

"What are you talking about?"

"Devon. There's something fishy about him."

"You'll have to be more specific than that," she told him evenly.

He hesitated, then said, "Ask him what he was doing watching your apartment building this morning at dawn."

Lara felt a chill. "What?"

"I was driving by on my way to work. He was across the street from your building, watching it."

"You must have been mistaken."

"No. It was Devon; he is rather noticeable, you know. And he was watching your apartment building."

No, not Devon. Sanity reasserted itself quickly. Devon hadn't wanted to leave her alone in her apartment last night, not after someone had broken in. He had been worried about her. So he had guarded her, that was all. Watched over her. That had to be it.

Sanity? In an insane situation?

She fought the doubts desperately. He couldn't be her enemy, not Devon. He'd been *with* her when that truck had tried to run her down, and they'd been together while her apartment was searched. He couldn't have been responsible for those things. He had urged her to call the FBI—

But that would have been the natural response. And she would have wondered if he hadn't urged her to call the authorities, would have been suspicious if he hadn't. Besides that, what made her so sure there was only one enemy? The cartel could have sent two. Yes, two. One to shake her, the other to steady her. One trying to frighten her and the other offering a sympathetic shoulder and a willing ear.

The stakes were high if her father had indeed gathered damning evidence against the cartel. They wanted that evidence. And since they clearly believed she knew something, what better way to get the information out of her? Attack on two fronts, one overtly deadly and the other subtle and designed to appeal to a lonely, isolated woman.

Dear God.

"Lara? Hey, I didn't mean to—" Luke broke off, then added worriedly. "You're white as a ghost!"

She looked at him, feeling numb. In a voice that sounded quite calm to her own ears, she said, 'Thanks for the warning, Luke."

Clearly upset, he said, "Look, maybe there's a reasonable explanation."

"Yes. Maybe there is." And maybe not. Maybe the only explanation was the one ripping at her like a knife. "I—I think I'll go home." She looked across the stage and found the director. "Nick, are we finished for the night?" she called. She was proud of her voice; it was steady.

"Sure. Same time tomorrow."

"Lara—"

"I'm fine, Luke. See you tomorrow." Before he could say anything else, she turned away from him.

She continued, vaguely, to be proud of herself. Her legs worked steadily as they carried her into the wings and backstage. She was in control. At least until she reached the scarred old table. Devon was sitting there, apparently studying his lines. Ching was curled up in his lap.

Purring.

Lara picked up her script and fished in the pocket of her jeans for her car keys. With utter calm, she said, "May I have my cat? I'm leaving."

Devon looked up at her, his eyes immediately narrowing. He rose, still holding Ching. "I'll carry him out to your car," he said slowly. "He's heavy."

She acceded to that only because she didn't trust herself to say another word without revealing the turmoil inside her. Silently, she led the way to the rear exit and outside. Unconsciously drawing deep breaths in the chilly night air, she walked to her car and opened the door, waiting for him to put the cat inside. When he silently did so, she got in and closed the door. She couldn't close him out, though, because the window on the driver's side was down several inches, and she heard him clearly.

"Lara, what's wrong?"

She inserted the key and turned it. The engine made a healthy getting-ready-to-start sound, but wouldn't catch. Lara waited a moment, then carefully held the gas pedal halfway down with her foot and tried again. Just the whirring of an engine that wasn't going to start. She tried again, and again.

"Damn," she whispered.

Opening the car door, Devon said, "Come on, I'll

take you home. You can call a garage tomorrow to have a look at it."

"I'll call a cab," she said tensely.

There was a moment of silence, and then he took her arm and pulled her from the car. His grip was neither painful nor rough, but she didn't think she could easily pull away from him.

"Ching," he said, waiting until the obedient cat joined them outside the car. He reached in for the keys, then shut the door and led Lara to his own vehicle. When he opened the passenger door, the cat leapt in without waiting to be told.

Lara wasn't given a choice; she was thrust unceremoniously inside. She didn't fight him, mainly because she was trying desperately to convince herself that she was imagining things, letting her suspicions run away with her. Devon wasn't her enemy; he *couldn't* be.

There was this affinity between them. And even though he was obviously fighting it, there was desire. It was real. They both felt it. He couldn't have faked that . . . could he? Could he be ruthless enough to pretend desire—or use it—just to get information from her?

No, he couldn't do that, because she . . . Oh, dear God.

Devon didn't say a word during the drive to her apartment, and when they got there he didn't give her a chance to escape him. He turned off the motor and then scooped up Ching somewhat brusquely, an action the cat protested with only a faint murmur. Then Devon got out of the car and came around to her side. She was already standing on the pavement.

"I can—"

"We have to talk," he said flatly. He took her arm and led her toward the building.

Minutes later, facing him in the living room of her apartment, Lara could feel her precarious control faltering. "There's nothing to talk about," she said, watching as he set Ching absently on the coffee table, shrugged out of his light jacket, and tossed it onto the couch.

"No? You walked offstage looking like somebody had kicked you in the stomach. You look worse now."

"Thanks," she said stiffly.

Devon shoved his hands into his pockets and stared at her, his eyes narrowing. "You heard something," he mused slowly, almost to himself. "Or were told something. What was it, Lara?"

Refusing to be in limbo again, Lara wanted answers. Good or bad, she had to know. "Nothing much. Why were you watching this building last night?"

He went very still. "Who told you that?"

"Never answer a question with a question."

"Tell me, dammit."

"You first. Answer the question, Devon."

"You should know the answer." His voice was impatient. "You wouldn't call the police or anybody else. Did you expect me just to leave tamely? Whoever searched this place could have come back. I watched in case they did."

"Knight errantry?" She wanted to sound mocking, but her voice emerged unsteadily.

Devon's lips twitched suddenly, and he said in a dry tone, "No, you forget. I'm the prince. I could have used a couple of squires, though. It was cold as a witch's broomstick out there last night."

Her suspicions wavered. That *voice* of his . . . And she didn't want to believe he was her enemy.

"Who told you, Lara?"

Automatically, she answered. "Luke. He saw you around dawn as he was passing by."

"Luke," Devon said softly.

Lara hardly heard him. "You could be lying. How do I know you aren't?"

"Why would I?" he demanded, and then frowned in a sudden realization. "Oh, I get it. I've suddenly become one of the bad guys."

"How do I know you aren't?" she repeated. "Nobody bothered me until I met you—"

"Nobody bothered you until they found you. Dammit, Lara, you met several people when you met me. You joined a community theater group. And I was with you when you were nearly run over; have you forgotten that?"

"No." She swallowed hard. "But there could be two people—one trying to frighten me, the other . . ."

"What? Trying to seduce you?" Devon's mouth tightened. "If I'd been on that end of the plan, we would have been lovers last night."

Lara didn't know what to believe; all her emotions were in turmoil. She felt so raw that a touch would have sent her screaming. "Maybe that's what you've been fighting," she heard herself say thinly. "It wouldn't be so hard to pretend desire, but there comes a point when it has to be real."

He stared at her for a long moment. A muscle bunched under the tanned flesh of his jaw, and his eyes were so dark they were nearly black. Then, in a thickened voice, he said, "It is real. That's the problem."

For a fleeting instant, Lara felt a feathery chill of fear. Because it would no doubt be a problem for a would-be assassin to feel real desire for his intended victim. But then, caught in the tortured shadows of his eyes, she saw and accepted the utter certainty that this man was no killer.

She half-lifted her hands in a pleading gesture. "Devon, I don't understand."

He hesitated, then slowly crossed the space between them to stand before her. "Lara . . ."

The last scrap of her control deserted her. "Dammit, tell me what's going on!"

Silently, he pulled a leather folder from his pocket, opened it, and held it out.

There was an ID card on one side, with his photo and name.

On the other side was a badge.

Five

At first, Lara was aware of nothing except the irony of it. At no point had it even crossed her mind that Devon could have been a federal agent. She stared at the badge for an endless moment, then turned away and went to sit on the couch. By the time he joined her there, she was beginning to think again.

"Why?" she asked.

He didn't need the question clarified. "More classified designs have disappeared," he said in an impersonal tone. "It began to look as if your father was right about some organized group's being behind the thefts. But we didn't have a lead. Then we received an anonymous tip—maybe from the same person who warned your father—that you were no longer safe."

"So you were sent here." She looked at him. "But undercover. I wasn't warned. What was I supposed to be, Devon? Bait?"

He didn't flinch from her steady gaze. "Yes, if

necessary," he answered softly. "The consensus was that you were the only chance we had."

Lara drew a breath. "You guys play rough."

"I won't try to justify that decision, Lara."

"Was it your decision?"

He hesitated, then shook his head. "No."

She realized, suddenly, what he had said. *If necessary.* And a bitter pang went through her. She had been right, in a sense. There *had* been two. On different sides, yes, and using radically different approaches—but sharing at least part of a goal: They both wanted information from her.

"The music changes," she murmured painfully, "but the dance is the same, after all."

"What?"

"So I was going to be bait *if necessary?*" She laughed with no humor. "The FBI didn't believe I'd told them everything; they made no secret of it. They thought I was holding something back. And they sent you to try once more to find out what it was. Is that your role at the bureau, Devon? Resident seducer?"

"No." His voice was bleak, and his shadowed eyes never left hers. "I was supposed to try and win your trust, I won't deny that. I can't. But what happened between us wasn't part of the plan."

Lara forced herself to look away, fixing her gaze on the cat still sitting on the coffee table and regarding them solemnly. "Right," she said. "Well, I guess you have to say something like that. After all, hope springs eternal. I just might be desperate enough not to give a damn why you're here."

"Don't, Lara."

"You'll have to forgive me." She kept her voice

detached and polite. "I'm afraid I don't know my lines. Outrage, maybe? Betrayal? Or should I just be quite pathetically grateful to have been treated like a mindless pawn?"

"You could have called the bureau at any point," he reminded tautly. "I urged you to—against orders, I might add. If you had done that, you would have been given a choice. To be hidden again, or to stay put. You had already made the choice, Lara. You didn't want to run."

"But I didn't know I was being used as bait! You should have told me. Why didn't you tell me?" It hurt that he hadn't been honest with her. She had broken all the rules to confide in him, while he had remained silent.

Devon took a deep breath and then spoke steadily. "I'm an undercover agent. I'm *always* undercover on an assignment. You said I couldn't know what it felt like to forget part of my life, my identity. To answer to a strange name. I do know what it feels like, Lara. I've known what it feels like for ten years. And in all those years, I never broke my cover. I never once told anyone who and what I really was, in large measure because my life depended on my playing the role I'd been assigned."

No wonder he had played the role of prince so convincingly; he was doubtless a natural actor, something the bureau had taken advantage of. And those past "roles" had, in all likelihood, been high-wire acts in deadly situations. She understood that, and the rationality of his defense made some of her bitter anger fade. But not all of it. "I wasn't your enemy," she whispered.

"I know. I'd already made up my mind to tell you

tonight—whether you believe that or not." He sounded tired.

"Why now?" Her voice jerked. "Because charm wasn't working?"

There was a moment of silence, and then he said, "We aren't lovers."

Her heart seemed to turn over inside her, and Lara was dimly aware that it was a purely intuitive response to his statement, as if something within her understood everything he meant with those three simple words. She tried to tell herself that she was seeing only what she wanted to, believing what her heart demanded that she believe. And yet . . . She felt that odd tug, the pull of something stronger than she was, and the power of the bittersweet affinity she felt with him almost stole her breath. She didn't look at him. Instead, all her other senses came tautly alive.

"I noticed," she said flatly. "So?"

"We could have been. You can't deny that." His voice was harsh now—and hard. "We should have been. And if I was an agent who just wanted to use you, for bait or anything else, we would have been. I wanted information from you, right? I wanted you to tell me everything you know about the night your father died, even the memories you can't bear to remember. And seduction would have given me that. So we should have been lovers."

"You were being noble?" she mocked with an effort that she hoped didn't show.

"It would have been the easy way, Lara. The quickest way. Just let nature take its course, and then listen to the pillow talk. And I *was* tempted."

She turned her head jerkily and looked at him.

His face was drawn, his eyes glittering in a way she'd never seen before.

Devon nodded. "Oh, yes, I was tempted—and not only because I wanted you so badly that I was half out of my mind. I was tempted because you wouldn't run, and you wouldn't hide, and I knew damned well you wouldn't panic. They wouldn't get any information from you, and I knew they'd have to kill you. So I was very tempted to take the quickest way to get the answers I needed from you."

"But you didn't." It was little more than a whisper.

"I couldn't do that to you. To us." He rose abruptly from the couch and moved away with the stiffness of a man who was rigid with control or pain. "I wish I could say it was nobility, but it wasn't. I simply didn't want you to hate me." Halting with half the width of the room between them, he faced her and shrugged wearily. "There aren't any princes, Lara, except in books and on stages. The rest of us simply do the best we can."

He waited, feeling as tense as if he'd just bet his life on a very dark horse. He half-expected her to order him to leave both her apartment and her life. She had bitterly referred to herself as a pawn, and he knew what she meant, knew how she must feel about that. But he couldn't go back and change the decision that had brought him into her life, any more than he could repeat these last few days.

And he couldn't expect a betrayal—even an incomplete one—to arouse in her anything but pain and disgust.

She rose from the couch and came slowly toward him, and when she spoke it was in a voice he'd never heard from her before. A voice that reached inside him and touched something that had forgotten what a gentle, understanding contact felt like.

"I couldn't hate you, Devon, even if I wanted to. I realized that tonight, when I thought you might turn out to be an enemy. And you didn't trick your way into this prison of mine. You knew the way because you've been here or in a place very like this. I've known that all along. That's why I've never been able to fight the way you made me feel."

He didn't move when she stopped an arm's length away. "And I know," he said reluctantly, "that prisons are lonely places. Don't misinterpret your own feelings, Lara."

"Is that what you believe I'm doing?"

"I think it's possible. Maybe even likely."

She looked up at him for a long moment, then said somewhat dryly, "I've been fighting this as hard as I know how. But it hasn't done any good. I don't believe in princes, Devon. And I don't know so much about happy endings. But I've never felt the way I do with you. And that's enough."

"The situation—"

"No, it isn't that." Lara hesitated, but knew this had to be resolved now. Steadily, she said, "I'm not in the habit of misinterpreting my own feelings, and being in a . . . prison hasn't changed that. I know how I feel. What I don't know is how you feel."

"You know."

"No." She smiled ruefully. "I don't know. It could have been the role."

He matched her smile, even though the strain showed through. "I'm *not* the resident seducer at the bureau. That was never the plan, I swear to you. I haven't been playing a role, Lara. Not when I've held you. Not when I've touched you." His voice hoarsened on the last few words, and he cleared his throat. "We can talk about that later. I—"

"We don't need to talk anymore." Lara had often been impulsive, and sometimes reckless, but she knew that neither of those emotions was driving her now. The timing was all wrong, she knew, because Devon was half-convinced it was the situation and not he who had sparked desire. But the certainty she felt went too deep to allow doubts to stop her.

"Lara—"

She took his hand and turned toward the hallway.

His fingers closed almost convulsively over hers. "Honey, you can't be sure," he said huskily.

"I can't be sure of much," she admitted softly. "But I am sure of this, Devon. Very sure." And she led him down the hallway to her bedroom.

"Yah," Ching said softly. He jumped onto the couch and trampled methodically on Devon's jacket until it was comfortably creased and folded. Then he turned around several times and curled up in a boneless ball with his ringed tail covering his nose. He murmured for a while in the back of his throat, the monologue holding a considering tone, then drifted off to sleep.

He dreamed about chasing rabbits.

"You're living for today," Devon said as she turned on the lamp by her bed and faced him. "Lara . . ." His haunting voice was deep and rough, his expression taut.

"And you know what that feels like," she said, tacitly confirming his assertion. Then she smiled. "But, Devon, it doesn't matter. Because if I knew, with absolute certainty, that a million tomorrows were waiting for me, it wouldn't change what I want tonight."

"How can you know—"

"I love you."

His breath caught with a harsh sound, and his eyes blazed with a sudden fire. He didn't question the words, or deny them, even though the part of him that was an experienced agent urged him to. He accepted, because he needed her too badly to doubt the astonishing generosity that could allow her even to say that to him.

Whether it was true or not.

He reached for her slowly, but the instant his hands touched her shoulders something inside him seemed to break. It was all he could do to force himself not to crush her in his arms, not to hold on to her with all his strength, as if some incoherent fear within him whispered that she'd be wrested away from him.

Lara melted against him, her arms sliding up around his neck, face lifting as he bent his head and captured her mouth with his. She felt a shudder go through his powerful body, and her own body trembled responsively. Her mouth opened to him eagerly, and a jolt of pure, raw desire seared her when his tongue touched hers. She had never felt anything like this mindless, compulsive need; it was as if she *had* to obey an instinct so ancient there was no name for it, there were no words for it.

She rose on tiptoe, fitting herself more firmly to

his hard body, and the sudden, throbbing emptiness in the deepest part of her yanked a sound from her throat that was almost anguish. The urgency that swept over her was very nearly madness, and her fingers shook uncontrollably as she began fumbling with the buttons of his shirt.

"Lara," Devon said raspily against her throat, his hands sliding down to curve over her bottom and hold her tightly against the swelling fullness of his loins. But she wasn't close enough, and a groan escaped him. Swiftly, he moved her away, caught the hem of her sweater, and drew it up over her head. The moment her arms were free, Lara's hands returned to his shirt, and she coped feverishly with the final button just as he unfastened her bra and pulled it off.

When she pushed the shirt off his shoulders, Devon shrugged out of it, his gaze fixed on her. The bulky sweaters she usually wore had allowed only a hint of the ripe curves beneath, and the utter perfection of her round, full breasts took his breath. The firm mounds filled his hands, nipples rising stiffly into his palms in an unbelievably sensuous caress. He heard her gasp, saw her vivid green eyes widen, darken, and she swayed toward him.

Devon was barely aware of a growl rattling in his throat. It was the sound of a caged wild thing. His senses flared violently as the hunger inside him reached a sudden, critical peak, and the part of his mind still capable of thought realized that he couldn't control this need for her. For an instant he quite literally couldn't move, didn't dare try because he was afraid the primitive beast inside him would burst free.

Then Lara's darkened gaze met his, and he realized that somehow, against all reason, she had been hurled into the same frenzy that gripped him. It was there, in her eyes, a fire every bit as hot as the one that burned him. He felt a kind of astonished wonder in her, matching his own, and he could move again.

Lara was so dazed by the storm of desire that she was only half-conscious of the rest of their clothing falling away. She didn't know who took off what and didn't care. No one had warned her that it could feel like this, that *she* could feel like this, the hunger so stunningly powerful that every nerve in her body was on fire with it.

He was kissing her urgently, lifting her and placing her on the bed, and she could only hold on to him desperately. And even though the sensations ripping through her were alien, they were also, somehow, familiar. Her body knew how to respond to his touch, as frantic as his own body; she was conscious of an instinctive knowledge of what would please him, and didn't hesitate to touch him, caress him.

Lara felt wild, desperate, greedy. She couldn't be still, couldn't stop the sounds she heard escaping her. Her trembling hands slid over the hard muscles of his back and shoulders, and her body arched with a will of its own as he stroked her swelling breasts. She tried to catch her breath and couldn't, a moan blocking her throat, need burning her like a mortal fever.

His mouth was on her breasts, hot and hungry, his hands moving over her with a desire and skill that made her ache. There were things she wanted to say to him, but there was no room for them, no breath for them—no need for them.

And no time. The shattering tension within them built with a swift, relentless power that denied them time. Lara had never felt such blissful agony, and when his hand slid down over her quivering belly and gently cupped her, the ache intensified so sharply that it wrung a cry from deep inside her. She felt his fingers probing, stroking, and she knew without a shadow of a doubt that she was going to splinter into a million pieces.

Devon seemed to know as well. A rough sound escaped him; he spread her legs and moved between them, his body taut as he held on to the last ragged threads of control.

Lara didn't want control. It never occurred to her to be tense or to anticipate pain; despite the unfamiliar sensations he aroused in her, nothing had ever felt as natural, and as inevitable, as this. Her body accepted him with the same utter certainty.

There was only one surprise, and it delighted Lara. She'd had the vague notion that kissing and caressing were preliminary actions meant to arouse, were more or less reserved for foreplay, and that once the actual physical act of lovemaking began that would be forgotten. But Devon, she found, made love to her entire body with his entire body.

The need burned just as hot in him; the shattering sensual tension wound just as tightly, but it obviously wasn't enough for him to just satisfy physical desire. He didn't possess her, he became a part of her, until she had no awareness of two separate bodies. There was only this incredible striving in a white silence, and a peak of pleasure that was devastating.

Lara couldn't separate the following hours into specific interludes. Sated passion became, somehow, renewing passion that built again to a shattering peak. And again. And again. She knew there had been moments of total exhaustion, but then energy would flow into them, and exhaustion would be forgotten. It seemed there was too much need in them to be satisfied completely. She was, from time to time, conscious of astonishment and more than a little awe, but there was little room in her for coherent thought.

Sometime before dawn, one of the peaceful interludes became sleep. If Lara had been capable of thought by then, she would have fully expected to sleep for at least a year, because she was dimly aware of the sheer inability to move so much as a muscle. She had, however, reckoned without Ching.

"Prrupp?"

Conditioned by Ching himself to respond to her demanding feline friend, Lara forced one eye open and peered across the broad expanse of Devon's chest. The room was bright; though the drapes were closed, daylight penetrated, and the lamp on the nightstand was still on. Devon was on his back, holding her against his side with both arms, and she felt so utterly relaxed she wanted never to move.

Except her very peculiar cat wanted something of her, and patience wasn't one of his strongest traits. Ching glared at her, looking offended as only a cat can.

" 'Lo, cat," she murmured, yawning.

Ching's aqua eyes narrowed. "Yah," he said, and snorted. He expressed himself with such force that he nearly fell off the bed. The bed was big, but so was Devon; Ching didn't have much room for his somewhat ample behind.

"I can't," Lara told him, interpreting the cat's annoyance as a pointed dialogue concerning his late breakfast. "I can't move. You'll just have to wait, dammit." She kept her voice low.

Ching rang the bell on his collar. He didn't seem to move at all, and Lara had never figured out how he got the bell to ring.

"Don't do that," she said, faintly irritated. "It's weird. You won't starve, you know."

The bell tinkled again, and Ching added an emphatic "Yah!" to the sound.

"I'll feed you liver. You love liver. Just let me stay here a few more minutes."

"Yah!"

"Liver with egg. You love that even more."

"Yah!"

"Please. Have a heart. I'll buy you one of those cat seats to fasten to the window, and you can watch the birds without having to cling to the sash."

Ching considered, obviously tempted by the bribe, but then snorted.

"I don't know why the Egyptians ever worshiped cats."

Ching smiled at her, eerily wise. "Yah," he said softly.

Lara moaned in despair and burrowed closer to Devon's warm, hard side. "Go away," she muttered. "Can't you see I'm busy?"

91

The cat gazed at her for a moment, then glanced at Devon's unaware face. Then he lifted one striped paw and placed it gently on the man's bronze shoulder. Slowly, the paw tensed, until the sharp claws began to extend.

"All right," Lara said hastily. "I'll get up. Stop that this minute!"

Ching's smile curled at the ends. He relaxed his paw.

Lara realized that her pillow was shaking, and lifted her head to stare down at Devon. Obviously, he was awake. Sapphire eyes glinted at her with a kind of enjoyment she'd never seen in him before—absolutely unshadowed.

Chuckling, he said, "If I told anybody that I was awakened by a two-sided conversation between you and your cat, I'd be locked up. Especially if I claimed to understand what Ching said in his part of the dialogue."

"Did you?" she asked curiously.

"Yes. He wanted his breakfast. And when you told him he'd have to wait, he decided to wake me up. Rudely."

"He's a strange cat," Lara admitted.

"Yah," Ching agreed complacently.

Devon looked at him for a moment, then said, "Excuse us?"

Ching returned the steady gaze, then muttered to himself and jumped down from the bed.

"I'll have to feed him, or he'll shred something."

Devon's arms tightened around her. "In a minute."

Lara, somewhat surprised to find that she felt no shyness at all after a definitely incredible night-before, smiled at him. "Good morning."

"Good morning." He kissed her, his morning beard a sensuous rasp against her flesh. "I was afraid I'd dreamed you," he said huskily.

She searched his expression a bit hesitantly. "No regrets?"

"No." The response was reassuringly instant. But then Devon frowned. "Except I didn't even think about protecting you, honey."

"The timing's wrong, I think," she said, reasonably sure, since she'd just finished her cycle.

He half-nodded, accepting that. "Still, we'd better be more careful from now on."

Though she hadn't believed that Devon intended only a one-night fling, she was relieved by the comment. "I'm all for planned parenthood," she told him.

"So am I." His eyes darkened slightly. "I don't want anything to push you into a decision you aren't ready for."

Lara smiled and kissed him, no longer startled by her strange understanding of him. "Just me?" she asked gently.

Devon hesitated, then sighed. "I want to make promises, Lara. But I can't even think past today. I can't *let* myself. Do you understand?"

"The way steeplechase jockeys make plans only after the last race. Like that?"

"Yes. Until you're no longer in danger, and all the questions are answered." His darkened sapphire gaze searched her eyes restlessly. "Until this is over, you won't be able to think clearly about your future."

She didn't know if Devon loved her. She knew that he felt the same bond she did, but whether that would prove to be a blessing or a burden to him remained to be seen. And she knew that she had no choice but to wait and find out.

Using one finger to draw an intricate design among the black hairs on his chest, she said calmly, "I know that. Or, at least, I know that you believe that. And I understand. Are you going to move in here with me for the duration? It *would* be safer, you know."

He smiled a little. "Safer for whom?"

"Me." She looked at him innocently. "Since my prince is also an FBI agent, he should certainly make it his responsibility to guard my body."

One of Devon's hands slipped beneath the covers and found a rounded hip. Gravely, he said, "Quantico instructs agents in all the latest techniques."

'So you're . . . um, up on those?"

"Couldn't you tell last night?"

"Was *that* what you were doing? Guarding my body?"

"I was using the definition of 'watchful care.' "

"Quantico teaches selective definitions too, huh?"

Devon cleared his throat. "There are expected to be a certain number of judgment calls in any situation. Last night, I *judged* that the best way of guarding your body was to remain very, very close."

"I approve." It was her turn to clear her throat as that wandering hand began to make interesting forays. Somewhat weakly, she added, "You can't!"

Injured, he said, "I've had at least four or five hours of rest, and—"

From the living room came the sound of a thunderous crash and a feline wail of surprise and rage.

Before Devon could do more than tense in response, Lara was giggling. "I got him!" she said gleefully.

"Ching? What'd you do to him?"

"The last time he got mad at me, he decided to shred the living room drapes, and since he has claws like steak knives, he can do a lot of damage. He knew I was furious, and *I* knew he'd try it again because cats love a strong reaction. After I replaced the set he ruined, I loosened the rod at one end; I figured his weight would bring the whole thing crashing down on him."

Devon listened for a moment, hearing a bitterly profane monologue coming from the living room. "It obviously worked," he murmured. Then he looked at Lara, and his lips twitched. "What have I let myself in for?"

She laughed and kissed him, but wiggled away before it could get interesting again. "I'd better go feed him, before he starts on the couch . . ."

Much later, after a shower that got quite interesting and a belated breakfast, which Devon cooked very well, Lara had a sudden dreadful thought. She hastily closed the dishwasher and went out into the living room, where Devon was rehanging the drapes and making sympathetic noises to the disgusted cat, who was sitting on the coffee table watching him.

"Could this apartment be bugged?" she whispered.

"It isn't," Devon said in his normal voice. He gave the drapes a last tug to make certain they were secure, then turned to her with a smile. "I had it checked yesterday, and again last night."

Lara sat down on the couch and thought about that. "I wish you'd told me sooner," she said finally.

"I suddenly realized that it could have been, and that someone could have been listening to us all this time. It was . . . unnerving."

He joined her on the couch. "I would have told you last night, but things started happening rather quickly and I forgot."

She was still thinking about it. "The apartment could only have been checked when I was with you. So you aren't alone here?"

"Not now. I called in backup after someone broke into this place. As a matter of fact, they're out pruning the bushes now."

Lara blinked. "That landscaping service?"

"Right. That's their cover during the day. At night, they're close as well. Four agents. Someone's always watching this building, and someone's always watching you."

"You really believe I'm in danger, don't you?"

Devon reached out to smooth a strand of silky blond hair away from her face. "I really do. Lara, last night before we left the theater, I checked your car. The steering mechanism had been tampered with. I made sure the engine wouldn't start."

She waited for fear to sweep over her. But it didn't. In her mind was the rational awareness that someone very likely wanted her dead, but . . . It was only then that Lara realized she no longer felt alone. For the first time in too many long months, that overwhelming sense of isolation was gone.

"Lara?"

She wanted to throw her arms around him and laugh out loud, because even living on the edge of a knife felt wonderful with the loneliness gone. It felt *alive.* Looking at him, she was conscious of a wave of love so powerful that it stole more than her breath for a moment. She didn't voice the feeling, because she knew Devon would think it was gratitude. He already thought that at least partly, she knew.

Instead, she drew a deep breath and said steadily, "So what's the next step?"

The shadows were back in his beautiful eyes for the first time that day. "I want you out of it," he said.

"You know better than that."

He did, and the reluctant knowledge was in his eyes, along with that almost savage anger that she'd seen before. But he said, "We'll find another way to get them, Lara."

"There is no other way. If I disappear, whoever they sent to get me will disappear as well. The only way is somehow to get the man they sent—"

"Or find your father's evidence."

"I don't know where it is!"

Devon put an arm around her. Quietly, he said, "You know something. I don't think you're holding back; I believe you know something you're not aware of."

"How could that be?"

He was silent for a moment, then said, "The mind plays tricks on us, honey. Especially when we've had a shock."

Lara shook her head. "But why would I block out some knowledge of where the evidence is?"

"I don't think that's it. I think you saw or heard something that you just didn't take in at the time."

"What?"

He looked at her gravely. "We can try to find out. If you can bear to relive that night."

"Hypnosis?"

"No, something similar. The mind retains every-thing, but sometimes you have to take it step by step through an experience in order to remember."

Step by step . . . Lara remembered telling Devon about that night, remembered the pain she'd felt. And everything inside her shied away from confronting those memories again. In the blur of images, all she could see clearly was her father's body.

She shook her head. "No. I—I can't. Not now, Devon, please. Not yet."

His arm tightened around her. "All right. But you'll have to face it sooner or later."

Lara forced lightness into her voice. "Not if we catch my would-be assassin."

"They sent a pro, Lara; you can be sure of that."

"Meaning that he won't be caught so easily?" She sighed. "I assumed as much. But so far his attempts have been at a distance and haven't involved guns. The truck, my car. If he's just trying to scare me—"

"In both cases, you could have been killed."

Lara thought about it, then began musing aloud. "Either he was following me that first night, or he knew where I'd be. He could have gotten to my car any time, I guess; but how did he know when the apartment would be empty long enough for him to search it?"

Devon gave her an odd look. "You were ready to think I was the man; hasn't it occurred to you that several other people entered your life at the same time you met me? People who are also involved in the play, who know where you are every night, where your car's parked."

After a long moment she said, "You think it's Luke."

"I think it could be."

Lara tried a laugh that didn't quite come off. "But he's funny, charming. He's not a killer."

"Honey, the most charming man I ever met was an international assassin."

"I just can't believe it."

He drew a short breath, then said softly, "He told you I was watching this building yesterday at dawn."

"Yes."

"How did he know it was your building?"

Six

Lara didn't want to believe it. She liked Luke, and facing the possibility that he could be trying to kill her was both difficult and chilling. "Nick has my address. Luke could have asked him about it."

"Yes. He could have. He's been interested in you from the first night." Devon sighed. "Maybe it's that innocent. And maybe he's just a talented carpenter moonlighting at a community theater."

"But?" she prompted, knowing there was more.

Devon was trying to keep his mind on business, and it wasn't easy. Despite the deadly situation surrounding Lara, memories of holding her in his arms kept distracting him as if it had been days instead of only hours since he had held her. It was an unexpected reaction, and his realization that their lovemaking had only added fuel to an already raging fire was more than a little unnerving.

That had never happened to him before. He wrenched his mind back to the most vital subject, refusing himself the luxury of exploring his own confusion.

"But. He's new in town and staying at a hotel. His regular job is a recent one, and the builder who hired him knows nothing about him except that he's skilled in the work. He doesn't seem to have a past, at least none that we could find; the car he drives is registered in his name, but the address is a post office box in California."

"California? He said that he was something of a gypsy at the moment." Lara shook her head. "But he *is* a skilled carpenter; would an assassin be able to fake that?"

"Who says he'd have to? Maybe it's his hobby. It isn't that unlikely. Lara, many paid killers lead perfectly normal lives most of the time. They command a high wage and often accept no more than three or four assignments in any given year. Some collect art or run legitimate businesses. As a general rule, the only traits assassins must have are the ability to consider murder just a job to be done and the detachment to do the job."

Devon watched her intently, wishing that he could insulate her from some realities that most people were never aware of. But he couldn't. She had to know for her own protection. He watched the acceptance of hard realities show on her delicate face, and it hurt him that she had to consider the motives and abilities of paid killers.

Lara shivered.

"Sorry, but you need to know." He forced a smile and held his voice steady. "Killers aren't all steely-eyed machines, or monsters with hate burning inside. You've probably passed a few on the streets with no more than a glance."

She was silent for a moment, then nodded. "Okay. Accepting the possibility that it could be Luke—has he guessed who you are, or was his warning just meant to keep a man from becoming inconveniently involved with me?"

"Good question." Devon frowned slightly. "If he *is* the one, we have to assume he's on to me—just to play it safe. But, at the same time, I can't understand why he'd warn you if he thinks I'm an agent; there was every chance you'd tell me about the warning, and that would focus my attention on him—and it did, even though I was suspicious before. Suspicious but more than a little surprised. I didn't expect the cartel's man to be directly on the scene with you, not at first."

"Why not?"

"Because it breaks the usual pattern." He hesitated, then said carefully, "Assassins don't generally get close to their potential victims, and we have to assume he's just that. Men who'd be involved in something like the cartel would see a threat—and eliminate it immediately. They'd send someone to get rid of the threat and not waste time with scare tactics."

"But they did this time." Lara tried to think it through. "So they must be very sure that evidence against them *did* exist, and at least reasonably sure that I know something. They sent someone to try for the information, at least as a first step. But why didn't they just—" She swallowed, unable to complete the chilling thought.

She didn't have to. Devon reached for her hand

and held it gently. He didn't complete her question, but he did answer it in a quiet voice.

"They could have had you kidnapped, but that kind of action always leaves a trail, especially when the victim is in the witness protection program and under at least periodic observation. And they couldn't count on making you talk, no matter what methods they used; there's no such thing as a foolproof way to get information. It's been months, and they know you haven't talked to us or we would have moved against them. They must figure that either you have a very good reason for keeping quiet—and they may be afraid of blackmail—or you quite honestly don't know that you know something."

"Then why try to make me panic?"

"Self-preservation," Devon answered promptly. "On your part, I mean, as well as theirs. They're using a method least risky to them in the event that you know nothing, and a method that could very well work. Lara, the human mind is an amazing thing. Mental blocks exist because of pain or shock or an unwillingness to face something, but let the mind realize that a block is endangering you, and the chances are good that the walls will come down in a hurry."

She stared at him. "It hasn't worked."

"That's why I don't think it's a block."

"You believe it's something I didn't notice at the time."

"Right. If you'd either deliberately or unconsciously blocked something out, I think you would have known it by now."

"Do you think they realize that?"

"Whether or not they do, I believe they're too uneasy about your father's evidence to take the chance of removing you without making certain. Think about it, Lara. Suppose the cartel believes you're staying quiet for your own safety. If you did indeed have that evidence, it'd be a damned good insurance policy."

"You mean, I'd think they wouldn't bother me so long as I had something to hold over them? Something to bargain with?"

"Exactly."

Lara was silent for a moment, allowing that idea to reach a logical conclusion. "Then we have to use that."

Devon knew what she meant, she could see it in his eyes, but he asked anyway. "Use it how?"

It was her love and understanding of Devon rather than thoughts of herself that made Lara consider her next words carefully before speaking. She knew, without a single doubt, that despite his training and responsibilities, Devon wouldn't hesitate to whisk her away the instant he believed she was in real danger. She also knew that this situation was tearing at him, that the conflict between man and agent was as strong as ever and as unresolved.

The agent was working on an assignment and had the duty as well as the desire to gather evidence against a very dangerous group of criminals; the man was involved with a woman who was, in all innocence, a linchpin in that situation and terribly vulnerable because of it.

Devon knew there had to be an ending to the deadlock between the bureau, the cartel, and her, and yet the only means of breaking that deadlock endangered her. Whether he loved her or not, the bond between them was very real, and he was hurting because the agent had been taught to use every tool available—and the man couldn't use *her*.

He hadn't wanted to use her as bait even in the beginning, when she was a stranger to him, and he was determined not to now. He very obviously intended to help her to "relive" the night her father had died, primarily in order to avoid using her as bait. The problem was that Lara was convinced she knew nothing that would help him.

And where did that leave them? If Devon was forced to make the decision to use her as a lure to get evidence against the cartel, it could destroy him. She felt that with a certainty that wouldn't be denied. Yet, if he decided against using her, and chose to get her safely away into another life, that also could destroy him. Because Devon knew all about the pain of being imprisoned with no roots and a strange identity, and the burden of being the one to lock her into another prison might well be the one burden he wouldn't be able to bear.

Lara drew a deep breath and spoke carefully. "What we need is more time. Time to find out if I really do know more than I think I do about that evidence. Time to figure out a way to end this. Right?"

Devon's face was still, but his eyes were haunted. He had at least a good idea what she was going to suggest. "Yes."

She wanted suddenly to throw her arms around him and hold him, wanted to drive away the shadows in his eyes. But she couldn't. She *couldn't*. What she was about to suggest would undoubtedly add more shadows. And she had no choice.

"Then we have to stall," she said. "We have to

make the cartel believe that killing me wouldn't help them." She forced all the calm she could command into her voice. "So they have to think that I do have the evidence, and that I'm using it as an insurance policy."

"I'm sorry I brought it up. Even if we could make them believe that, it's too dangerous," Devon said immediately. Tightly.

"It will give us time. They'll have to rethink their options, decide how much they're willing to risk." She drew another breath. "Devon, I'm not running this time. I won't let anyone hide me away again. I can't be hidden if I don't want to. So unless you're prepared to put me in a real prison with real bars, you'd better accept that."

"Dammit," he said almost inaudibly.

Lara hurt inside, but she wasn't willing to back down. This had to be her decision, for both their sakes. She could only hope she was able to make him see and understand why; it was so important. "Besides that, what if I don't remember anything helpful? In that case, the only way to get at the cartel is to make them deal with me."

"They won't," Devon said roughly. "Their man knows I'm on to him, we have to assume that. And we have to assume they believe you've kept any knowledge about the evidence to yourself; otherwise the bureau would have moved against them by now. They'll decide very quickly to get you out of the way."

"Not if we make sure they believe that my death wouldn't stop the evidence from coming to light," she said.

Devon moved slightly, almost unconsciously, as if his whole body rejected the word "death." "How do we do that? Take out an ad in the classifieds warning the cartel that you've left the evidence with some nameless third party with instructions to reveal it if anything happens to you? Dammit, Lara, that's right out of a grade B movie!"

She smiled a little. "Yes, it is, isn't it? But I'm not a pro, Devon. I'm an amateur. A very scared amateur. All I know about the so-called underworld is what I see on television and read in novels. And from those examples, I know that any smart person with damaging evidence always protects himself that way."

He stared at her. "Are you seriously suggesting that you run an ad in the newspapers?"

"Why not?"

Drawing a deep breath, Devon spoke with careful restraint. "Which newspapers? And just what do you plan to say?"

Lara refused to let his obviously forced skepticism rattle her; she knew where it was coming from. "Since I'd have to be an idiot not to have realized somebody's after me right here in Pinewood, I'll run it in the town daily. And then—"

"Assuming a hired killer would take the time to read the newspaper?"

"He will if he knows I went to the newspaper office. And I would assume it was only logical that he was following me, wouldn't I?"

More or less cornered on that point, Devon visibly gritted his teeth. "And then?"

"The New York and D.C. papers; Dad and I lived just outside Washington."

That was too rational for Devon to protest; the New York papers tended to monitor the pulse of the entire country, and D.C. was close enough to home-ground to be reasonable. Before he could find an objection somewhere, Lara went on in the same calm, reflective voice.

"As to what I should say in the ads, I'm not quite sure. Something to catch their attention, certainly. They'll have to believe that I know I'm being stalked, and that I've protected myself by leaving the evidence with someone they couldn't possibly know about."

"Lara—"

Frowning thoughtfully, she interrupted. "And we'll have to get you innocently out of the way when I place the ads, or the cartel's man will think you know what I'm doing. Even if he's not sure you're an agent, he'll smell a trap. It has to look like you're still trying to get information from me and I'm not giving any. Or that you're definitely not an agent. Damn. This is getting hideously complicated. I'll bet he knows you spent the night here."

Devon swore under his breath, being quite creative, and then said somewhat fiercely, "Even if they get the message and *don't* smell a trap, what d'you think they'll do, Lara? Turn tail and run?"

Gently, she said, "No. I think that eventually they'll try to grab me."

After a long and tense moment, he said, "I won't let you do it. There has to be another way."

"There isn't, and you know it." She lifted her free hand to touch his taut cheek. "Devon, you said yourself that there couldn't be any talk of futures until this is over. I don't even *have* a future, not with this hanging over me. It has to be resolved, one way or another. I want the men who stole secrets and killed my father punished, and I want to be free to live my life as *I* choose to live it. Not in a prison of any kind, not under a threat—and not in limbo. I won't be satisfied with anything less, no matter what the risk."

Devon almost yanked her into his arms, pulling her across his lap and holding her tightly. In a voice with all the feeling squeezed out of it, he said, "Don't you understand that I can't keep you safe here if they really go after you? No matter how many people are with you and watching you, if they try hard enough to get at you, they can. Somehow."

"I know that." Lara smiled up at him, using every ounce of her willpower to ignore the strong thighs beneath her. But even now, with the tautness of other emotions between them, she was conscious of a desire so powerful, the sound of it ached to escape her throat. She held her voice steady. "But if we play this just right, we can trap the man they sent after me before they've made up their minds to grab me."

Still holding her, he winced slightly. And there was even a flash of reluctant humor and unwilling admiration in his burdened eyes. "Dammit, what've you got in mind?"

Lara forced herself to concentrate. She was still putting the plan together mentally, but she didn't intend to tell Devon that. "Well, it's going to be very complicated—"

"So I guessed. In case it didn't occur to you, I've read your file. I know what your IQ is. Any plan you come up with is *bound* to be complicated."

"My father was generous with his genes," was her only comment on that.

"Something the cartel is certainly aware of. So

don't think you can play dumb with them," he warned.

"That's not what I had in mind." She was relieved that he had decided to hear her out. Not that she expected him to like what she was planning, but he was too intelligent himself not to realize eventually that it was the only way. At least she hoped so.

"What *do* you have in mind?"

"First, we agree that the cartel believes there's a chance I'll panic?"

"It certainly looks that way."

"All right. Then suppose I make it fairly obvious to the cartel's watching man that the ads in the newspapers are partly a bluff. That I do know where the evidence is, but haven't safeguarded it by giving it to anyone else, mainly because I never got the chance. I've been more or less in protective custody since that night, remember. But I've kept quiet about the evidence because I've thought I might need to use it. Now the cartel has found me, and I'm scared. In that case, I might well use the evidence as a bluff, but I'd very quickly *try* to safeguard myself."

He frowned a little. "By getting word to someone?"

"No. By going back to the house outside D.C. and getting the evidence myself." The house had been closed up, but it was still hers. The FBI had been fairly confident they would find evidence against the cartel quickly, so they had allowed that; she had promised not to go near the place until she was told it was safe to resume her real identity. And despite the tragedy that had happened there, Lara had wanted a place to return to, a place that was a part of her past.

"They searched the house," Devon objected. "So did we—and very thoroughly."

"But they can't be absolutely positive the evidence isn't there, hidden in a place no one would find."

Devon saw the point and obviously wasn't happy about it. "And what would I be doing while you drive off to D.C.? If the cartel's man knows who I am—"

"How good is your cover?" she interrupted.

"The seams won't show unless he can dig a hell of a lot deeper than I think he can. But if he already suspects me, he won't risk believing I'm just an innocent bystander."

"Then we'll have to distract him. The cartel can't know the bureau was tipped that I was in danger, and even if their man suspects you, he has to be wondering why I haven't been spirited away by now."

"He could guess I'm undercover."

"Yes, and after what he told me last night—assuming it's Luke—he'd expect me to guess as well. He'd expect me to think either that you're FBI or that you're the one who's after me."

After a moment, Devon nodded slowly. "I see what you're getting at. I'm the potential bad guy again. You presumably call your contact at the bureau and report me as possible trouble, a couple of agents in three-piece suits show up somewhere public to have a little talk with me, and they leave me in the clear. A shell game."

"Right." From his expression, Lara knew that he thought it was a pretty good idea, even if he still didn't like it one bit. "Assassin or agent? The assassin knows who he is, and if he sees a couple of obvious agents dismiss you as no threat and then leave as quickly as they came—"

"I don't know you're in the program and don't connect the questioning with you? We'll have to come up with a good cover story as to why the agents question me."

She realized Devon was hardly aware that the agent in him had already accepted her plan as viable; but it was the man she had to convince, and she knew it. "Yes, something the cartel's man would believe. Then I'll have to seem to be relieved about you, but still worried that I'm in danger and not willing to involve you in my troubles."

"You wouldn't have told the FBI about the attempts against you so far? I don't know, Lara, that's pretty hard to swallow."

"I haven't told the FBI anything. I've told only you."

He acknowledged that point with a rueful nod, but didn't drop the objection. "But how do you convince the cartel's man that you've kept your mouth shut? The usual reaction of protected witnesses is to suspect anything that looks odd. You were almost run down by a truck, your apartment was searched, and your car was tampered with."

"He can't be sure that I know about the car yet," she pointed out thoughtfully. "No one was outside when we left the theater, and I have been riding with you."

"Granted. But it's a very fine line, Lara. You have to be suspicious enough to run the ads and try to protect yourself, and yet not scared enough to yell for help?" He was hoping to make her see reason, but a coldness deep inside him warned that Lara had already made up her mind.

After a moment she said, "I hope I'm a good enough actress."

He knew she wasn't talking about her part in the play *Rapunzel.* "How good?"

"Good enough to very subtly convince everyone at the theater that I have a strong—but mysterious—dislike of the FBI. If the cartel's man believes that, he just might be willing to believe that I'm determined to handle the threat myself."

"That's too many mights and maybes," Devon said flatly. The coldness inside him was growing, spreading out. God, didn't she realize that the chance she'd succeed was so slight, it was almost nonexistent? If a trained and experienced agent had suggested it, he would have been willing to try, because it *was* their best chance of getting at the cartel, at least as things stood now.

But not Lara. Not Lara.

"Can't be helped. And you know there's no other way." She was still hoping to convince him without resorting to the ace up her sleeve, because it would be a very painful card to play, she knew only too well.

Devon sighed roughly and held her a bit tighter. "Look, even assuming we have the time necessary for the cartel to read the ads, and even if we manage to convince everyone involved to believe what we want them to believe—what then? There'll no longer be any question that you're a threat to the cartel; they'll have to make their move, and fast."

If he could only make her realize . . .

"Then we set the trap." Quite deliberately she added, "With me as the bait."

"No." The word almost jerked out of him.

It was very difficult to sound cold and hard with a man whose lap one was lying across and with whom one had shared a rather extraordinary night-before in the bed just down the hall, especially with desire burning hotter with every passing second and her heart aching because this was hurting him, but Lara did her best. "Yes. For the first time since this situation started, I'm going to be in control of my own actions. Me, Devon, not someone else. Not even you."

He got her off his lap. "No."

Lara wasn't hurt by the physical withdrawal; he was just attempting to get back on his agent footing, and she knew it. She also knew that he would be forced to realize that she had already won the argument. The man could seduce reason and leave her virtually helpless if he chose, but the helplessness would only be temporary; and the agent couldn't fight the knowledge of a good plan when he heard one. Especially when it was the only solution.

"There's no other way. You have no evidence against the cartel's man. When he follows me to the house, you'll be waiting there."

"And you'll persuade him to confess while I hide somewhere and get it on tape? Not bloody likely."

She studied Devon's face for a moment. He had a look she recognized, even though she'd never seen him wear it before; it was a look of sheer, iron determination. There was only one way she knew to break through that resolve of his—and she didn't want to use it. Despite the strong affinity between them, their relationship was fragile in its very newness, and she was afraid that if she pushed him too far their bond would snap under the strain.

She could lose him.

And yet, what choice did she have? Two million years of evolution had instilled in the male half of humankind a protective instinct that no amount of intellect could erase; every iota of knowledge and experience Devon possessed, as well as his professional responsibilities, weighed virtually nothing in the balance.

Lara knew that. It wouldn't have been true of all men, but it was true of Devon. If she allowed him to, he'd fight all her battles for her. And especially this one, whatever it cost him—not because he thought her unable to fight herself, but because the bond between them, blessing or burden, made her a part of him somehow, a part he would never willingly endanger.

She sat back slowly on the couch and braced herself inwardly for what she had to do. "All right," she said quietly. "Then I'll call my contact at the bureau, and tell him what I have in mind. You know he and his group at the bureau will agree to it."

Devon drew a short breath, and when his vivid, haunted eyes searched her face Lara knew he was looking for any sign that she was bluffing. She also knew that he didn't find what he was looking for.

"I won't let you do that," he said evenly.

"You don't have the right to stop me. I haven't given you that right." Lara could feel something shift between them and almost held her breath. Her instincts told her that Devon would respect strength, but she wasn't sure if he could accept being backed into a corner; in that situation, *his* instincts would demand that he fight.

"Don't do this to me."

She got up from the couch, moving jerkily, and took a few steps away from him. It didn't help. The bond between them was a living thing, quivering tensely in the air, strained almost to the breaking point. It hurt her, pulled at her like nothing she'd ever felt before, and it would have been so easy to give in to him and stop the torment.

So easy. And so impossible.

She turned her back to him, feeling something hot on her cheeks. It was hard to see, but she wasn't looking at anything anyway, except something inside her where it was blurry too. The thick sound of her own voice startled her. "I have to. I won't let you tear yourself apart trying to decide. It's *my* decision. And I've decided."

She didn't expect what happened then, couldn't have anticipated it. For an instant, she felt the pain of being tugged sharpen almost unbearably. Even in her anguish, she was conscious of awe; she had known the strange bond of affinity they shared was a deep one, but until then she hadn't understood how complete it was. It was an empathic thing, and she felt his raw emotions as keenly as she felt her own. He was fighting, she realized, trying to draw back from her emotionally because it was instinct to shy away from being known so totally.

Then, suddenly, the dreadful pain eased and she could breathe again. He was behind her, his arms enclosing her and drawing her back against his tense body. He was swearing softly, his beautiful voice rough and shaken, the sound of it not quite defeat but something close.

It wasn't his pride or ego that had absorbed the blow she had dealt, but a deeper, more nameless thing. And he had given in, not because of her threat, but because of what his own struggle against that threat had done to them both.

Lara turned in his arms, her own going up around his neck. The chaos of emotions she felt were hers and his, wild and burning inside her. She *wanted* with a fury that was almost numbing, like something cut loose inside her. She wanted freedom for herself, her roots back and to choose the direction of her own life, wanted justice for her father—and, most of all, wanted Devon. He was in her heart, embedded more deeply than her soul, yet what she wanted most from him he hadn't offered and she couldn't ask for.

"All right." His voice was still shaken, he could hear it, and he could feel the aftershocks inside him. "All right, Lara." A part of him refused to believe what had just happened, yet he couldn't deny the inescapable reality of it; the lingering agony he felt was all too genuine.

With an adulthood of secrets and shadows at his back, the shock of realizing how certainly she defined—and felt herself—his emotions had caused him to withdraw automatically from her. Or, at least, try to. It had been like reaching the end of a rope after an abrupt fall, a wrenching halt that had quite literally knocked the breath from him and hurt like nothing he'd ever known before.

"You can't choose!" she said fiercely, staring up at him out of wet green eyes. "I won't let you."

Alone all his life, Devon couldn't quite believe in this. The affinity he had sensed with her he had assumed to be based on the loneliness they both felt, and the overwhelming passion they had shared seemed to spring from the same source despite her astonishing words of love. But not this, not this amazing tie that was a tangible thing. This was something else, something too starkly powerful to come only from loneliness.

"All right," he repeated, giving in because there was nothing else he could do; despite his doubts about the reality of this, he could see that his own struggles were hurting her as well as himself—and he couldn't hurt her.

He kissed her, needing to soothe the pain with a touch. If he had thought about it at all, he would have believed that the strange, raw emotions between them would have been a kind of barrier against desire, that only tenderness was possible at such a ruthless moment; but he was wrong. The dull ache of pain receded in a rush, like a wave retreating from the shore to make way for the next, and hunger washed over him.

"Lara," he murmured huskily against her lips. A throaty sound escaped her, and her eyes were darkening, fixed on his with wonder and need.

He lifted her into his arms without thought, carrying her down the short hallway to the bedroom. Just as it had been the night before, he felt a certainty in his inability to control this. And just as before, he felt the same uncontrolled hunger in Lara. He stood her by the bed long enough for their clothes to be flung aside, and there was a surge of almost savage delight in him because she was as eager as he.

Lara pressed her naked body against his, and her hands stroked compulsively over the solid muscles of his back, feeling them move under her touch.

Dear Lord, she wanted him so badly . . . It was like a craving in her soul. Her mouth explored his throat and shoulders and chest, glorying in the hard strength of his body, the warmth of it. All her senses expanded with a rush that was wildly exciting, until she was so acutely aware of him, it was as if only he existed. As if only he were real.

And her excitement built as she felt his response. His breath was coming as roughly as hers; his flesh was burning as if some mortal fever raged inside him, like hers; and she could feel his heart pounding in his chest, his powerful body shuddering as she touched him.

"How I want you," Devon muttered in a rasping voice, lifting her naked body easily into his arms.

Lara clung to him as he lowered her onto the bed and joined her. "Yes," she whispered, her throat aching as she stared up at his taut face, conscious of a sense of awe that she could make him want her with the almost desperate hunger she felt herself and saw reflected in his eyes.

She forgot the pain of before, forgot the sword hanging over her head and the dangerous, difficult times that certainly lay before her. She could think only of Devon and the feelings he roused in her. His mouth brushed between her breasts, then trailed fire across the flushed, swollen curves. His hands were caressing her body with sure knowledge, bringing every nerve ending wildly alive and quivering.

She was burning, aching with sweet torment that seemed to fill her consciousness until there was nothing else. Some part of her was aware that her body began to move against him, restless and wanting, her hands shaking as she held on to him with a rising urgency. "Devon . . ."

His mouth was on her breasts, moving with exquisite slowness as if he had all the time and patience in the world, driving her mad with his teasing. And yet his own body was taut and shaking, his handsome face fixed in a look of control that was almost masklike. And his eyes were blazing, the shadows burned away by a primitive inner fire.

Devon felt that fire intensely, roaring inside him, and some deep part of him recognized that only one emotion was powerful enough to fuel such an inferno. It was a bittersweet realization, because he was convinced that Lara's love for him, born in a prison, could not survive freedom.

In helping to free Lara, he would lose her.

Seven

Without even thinking about it, he followed his instincts. The bond between them was amazingly strong; he would do everything in his power to strengthen it even more. He wanted to fill her with himself, make her a part of him until she'd never be rid of him.

A growl rumbled in his throat as he held her shaking body firmly and kept a rigid grip on his own threadbare control. Lord, she was so beautiful, as wild in his arms as the emotions ripping through him . . . as necessary as his next breath.

"Devon." She moaned softly and tugged at his shoulders, desperate to feel him inside her. The spiraling tension was building unbearably until she thought she'd scream under the shattering force of it. He resisted her plea, teasing her aching breasts with fiery licks and maddening nibbles, letting her feel the sharpness of his teeth and the soothing touch of his tongue.

Wild with need, Lara instinctively fought his restraint with a seduction of her own. Her trembling hands moved over him, exploring hard muscles, tracing the straightness of his spine with just the tips of her fingers. She could feel him tense even more, heard another growl rumble from his throat, but it wasn't enough.

She slid one hand down his hard stomach, closing her fingers around him. She heard his hoarse gasp, and her own excitement spiraled violently as she felt the throbbing power of him, hot and rigid in her hand. She stroked him slowly, watching his vibrant eyes grow hotter, his face tighten in a spasm of pleasure that was almost agony.

Devon groaned raggedly, and his control shattered. Swiftly, he rose above her, slipping between her cradling legs and pulling them high around him. He thought he'd go out of his mind when her hot, moist flesh tightly surrounded him, and he buried himself in her with a primal need to merge their bodies completely.

Lara responded with all the fire he had ignited in her, accepting his almost savage passion with her own lithe strength and a consuming need that matched his. In her mind were words of love, cried out in silence, because the only sound she could make was a wordless whimper of searing pleasure.

Neither of them mentioned the strangely painful, silent struggle between them; Lara knew they weren't ready for that yet. Devon still had his doubts, and she knew that too. He hadn't mentioned her declaration of love even when he could have during their verbal argument.

You love me. Don't do this to me.

He could have said that, and she might well have lost. But he hadn't. And she had won.

If it could be called winning. Lara was afraid. She knew the odds were against her survival. The stakes were too high to allow the cartel the luxury of time to consider her fate; a dead possible threat would always be judged less trouble than a live one.

Much less trouble.

All she had as a bargaining chip was the elusive evidence against them. It might not exist, but she had to convince the cartel's lurking watcher that it did, and as quickly as possible. She had to remove all pressure from the watcher, convince him that he *had* the luxury of time and at least a chance of obtaining the evidence from her.

"It's been less than a week since the first move was made against you," Devon said thoughtfully as they planned that afternoon. "Maybe we can steal a few more days. It's chancy, though."

Lara was already counting on her acting abilities; she was being utterly matter-of-fact about the situation. "No more so than just waiting. At least this way, we'll give them all a few things to think about."

"Maybe too many things." Devon had given in because he had no choice about it, but he was using every ounce of his experience and intelligence to anticipate and plan for every possible reaction to the various threads of their strategy. His biggest concern was, of course, Lara's safety—and that was by far the most difficult certainty to ensure. "And I don't like your being out in the open."

"Just for a few minutes," she reminded him. "It's necessary. I'll have to go right away, otherwise he won't believe the agent has had time to get here."

"I have four men around you; one of them can follow you to the newspaper office."

"And he'd certainly notice I was being followed. He'll be looking for it. We can't let that happen, Devon." They were, she thought, risking a great deal just by assuming that the watcher was indeed watching. Because if he wasn't, their plan was ruined before they had even begun.

"There are people all over town today; he wouldn't notice anyone following you." He met her stubborn gaze for a long moment, then swore with more resignation than heat. "Dammit, will you let me at least *try* to protect you?"

Lara smiled a little. "You will. I'm counting on that. Look, the walk to and from the newspaper office will take no more than half an hour; it's only a few blocks away, and as you said, the sidewalks are crowded today."

Devon frowned at her, but he couldn't really disagree with her reasoning. If the cartel had intended a quick bullet to end the problem Lara represented, it would have acted days ago. Clearly the members of that cartel wanted to avoid drawing just the sort of attention an assassin's shot would provoke. And the same reasoning applied to the possibility of kidnapping; a grab in broad daylight on a crowded street tended to be noticed.

Especially in a small town.

Sighing, Devon allowed himself to be led to the door. He had to leave first in order to be blamelessly out of the way while Lara set the wheels in motion. And he had to set a few in motion himself.

"How long will you be?" she asked, showing the first sign of nervousness.

He pulled her into his arms. "A couple of hours, I think," he answered, hating the idea of being away from her even that long. He bent his head and kissed her thoroughly, and when she instantly responded he was aware that if he didn't leave soon, he wouldn't be able to.

"I'll be here," she promised in an unsteady voice.

That hope was too deeply rooted in him to be easily voiced. He simply nodded and left her. Outside the building, he paused almost imperceptibly on the steps and, without seeing to, directed a brief comment in a very low voice to one of the gardeners, who was busily spreading damp mulch around the roots of a prickly holly bush.

"She's leaving. No one follows her."

"Right," the gardener murmured.

Devon went to his car and got in, then started it and pulled away from the curb. He didn't look back. It was one of the hardest things he'd ever done in his life.

"You can't go," Lara told Ching firmly.

The cat, perched on the back of the couch, narrowed his eyes at her and said "Yah!" with an emphatic snort.

She looked at him musingly. He'd been amazingly tactful these last hours, not demanding attention of the preoccupied humans and remaining virtually silent.

"We'll be going to the theater in a few hours," she reminded him consolingly, getting her spare door key from the ledge above the door and sliding it into the pocket of her jeans. She picked up her purse, smiling a little as Ching muttered.

Then, squaring her shoulders, she went out and closed the door behind her. She paused outside the building on the steps, but hers was a more obvious hesitation than Devon's had been. Cautiously, she glanced around, presenting, she trusted, the appearance of a nervous woman wary of being watched —and more than half-certain she was being watched.

Only one gardener was at work, his back to her. He didn't appear to notice her.

She made a point of looking at her watch, then went on down the steps and along the sidewalk. She kept her pace brisk and her expression calm, but her eyes moved restlessly. It took no more than ten minutes to walk the distance to the newspaper office, and since her carefully worded ad was printed out in block letters on a sheet of paper in her purse, she was inside the office a bare five minutes.

Back outside again, she retraced her steps for one block, then stopped at a phone booth and placed a call. She did indeed call her contact at the FBI, explaining the situation rapidly in a low voice and telling him that Devon would be in touch with more details within the next hour or so.

Then Lara continued steadily down the sidewalk, distracting her mind from nervous thoughts of snipers or runaway cars by imagining what that faceless voice on the phone was like in person. A professional, certainly; he hadn't been the slightest bit rattled to hear that a protected witness had decided to take on her hunters and play a dangerous game of cat and mouse. He had been utterly calm, with a voice so unflappable and soothing that it should, she thought, have been used to record emergency messages in any situation where people were on the brink of panic.

Middle-aged, she decided; a voice that calm had to have been earned over decades. Salt-and-pepper hair and a face that had been lived in. Nice eyes. Comfortable padding layered over old muscle, but still a wicked backhand on the tennis court.

Lara stared at the doorway of her apartment building, blinked, and went slowly inside. It wasn't until she was in her apartment and leaning back against the closed door that she released a shaky sigh of relief.

"Prrupp?" Ching inquired, still sitting patiently on the back of the couch.

"We can't go back now, cat," she murmured. "Like it or not, we're in for the duration."

"Wauur," Ching said, and rang his bell.

She frowned at him. "I told you not to do that."

Ching smiled. Just like the Grinch.

"Devon?" Nick looked a bit startled. "There's a man here to see you. In my office. He said that Com-Tech suggested you might be here."

They had been about to run through a few lines, since Nick had made changes overnight, and Devon rose from his seat at the scarred table with a slight lift of his brows.

"Who is he?"

Nick cleared his throat. "He has a badge."

Devon looked even more surprised, and slightly amused. "I have an unpaid parking ticket; does the law in Pinewood usually track down citizens for that?"

"Um. An FBI badge."

His amusement died, and Devon just looked baffled. He hesitated, then shrugged and headed backstage toward Nick's office.

Sonia Arnold was the first to speak. "FBI? What on earth could it be about "

"I don't know," Nick offered. "He was very casual, even friendly. Just asked if he could speak to Devon for a few minutes. I didn't think it was my place to ask what it was all about, so I didn't."

"Maybe Devon will tell us," Melanie said hopefully.

"Only if he wants to," Nick returned in a warning tone. "Unless he's carted off in handcuffs, it isn't our business."

Melanie grinned. "It's definitely Lara's business; she won't want to kiss a known felon!"

Ching hissed at her. She had been sitting across from Devon, and the cat had very obviously put up with her presence in order to sit near his idol. However, now that Devon had left, Ching stood up and walked down the table to be near Lara.

She welcomed him with a frown for his bad manners, then looked at the others with a casualness that she hoped appeared a little tense. "I don't think they let known felons run around loose. Do they?"

"In a perfect world, no," Pat murmured.

"Let's not speculate," Nick begged. He looked behind Lara, who was sitting with her back to the stage, and said, "Luke, did your guys put the garden scene back onstage?"

"Yeah, it's ready," Luke returned cheerfully. "So's the inside tower room. The stage is crowded, and it looks peculiar, but both sets are there."

"Great. Sonia, Pat, you and Melanie come with me. I want to go over your marks for the first scene."

Lara remained where she was, her fingers idly toying with the pages of her script and her gaze fixed in the direction that Devon had taken to Nick's office. She was tensely aware of Luke's presence behind her, but didn't react to him until he came around the table and sat down with one chair between them.

"Lara?"

She blinked, then looked at him. This man could well be a cold-blooded killer, and the chill of that was inside her. But she kept her fear buried and with grim determination hung on to the role she was playing.

"Are you all right?"

"Of course. I'm fine." She allowed her lips to curve in a strained smile and her eyes to flicker again toward the distant office.

Luke wore a grave expression, his clear blue eyes concerned. "Fine? I can feel the strain, like last night. You were so upset last night. I was going to stop by your apartment, but—well, Devon's car was parked out front."

He had, she thought coldly, made a number of observations in a very few days. He knew where she lived, knew the car Devon drove. Since she was reluctant to say too much for fear of giving her true feelings away, Lara chose to remain silent, and merely looked at him.

His gaze fell first. "I know, it's none of my business. But he was watching your apartment, like I told you. And now there's an FBI agent talking to him."

A vague part of Lara's mind recognized that if Luke was indeed the cartel's man, he was one hell of an actor. He seemed so genuinely concerned, so worried about her. She felt the prickle of a doubt, but didn't let it alter her behavior; until there was proof to the contrary, she had to suspect Luke. She had to suspect virtually everyone.

She kept her voice steady, but allowed the tension to be heard. "As you suggested, there was a reasonable explanation for Devon's watching my apartment."

"Oh?" Luke was clearly doubtful.

"Yes. He was concerned about me. Let's leave it at that, shall we?" They had decided that Lara shouldn't be too forthcoming with information; she was unlikely to admit to anyone that her apartment had been searched, but both she and Devon hoped that Luke would assume that was what she meant.

Frowning, Luke said slowly, "I get the feeling it wouldn't have mattered much whether it was a reasonable explanation or not. But, Lara, the FBI. Doesn't it bother you?"

She let her gaze wander in the direction of the office again and smiled just a little. "You shouldn't worry about me, Luke. I'm careful. I'm very careful."

"Yah!" Ching said, his eyes fixed on Luke.

Luke met that inimical glare for an instant, then ignored the cat as he looked back at Lara. "Careful? You haven't known him a week."

"I haven't known you a week either."

He grimaced slightly. "Touché."

Lara rose from the table and smiled at him a bit absently when he rose as well. "Like I said—don't worry about me. I'm a big girl, all grown up and everything."

"No kidding." His tone was polite.

She started toward the stage. "No kidding."

"It's just because your cat likes him," Luke muttered, following her.

She felt a surge of warmth it was impossible to

fight as memories flashed through her mind. "No," she murmured. "Not because my cat likes him."

Luke must have heard something in her voice, because he didn't say anything else. Instead, with a rueful expression on his face, he went on past her as Nick hailed him.

She stood watching, realizing that Nick wasn't happy with the garden scenery and was ordering a great number of changes. Sonia and Pat were sitting patiently on a low "stone" garden wall as they waited for the director's attention to return to them, and Melanie wandered up to Lara a few minutes later.

"If you're through with that one," she said dryly with a nod toward Luke, "can I have him?"

Lara swallowed instinctive words of warning that she couldn't afford to offer and conjured a smile. "He isn't mine to give."

Melanie's dark eyes held a glimmer of laughter. "No? Just wanted to be, huh?"

"He's a charming man," Lara said diplomatically.

"But you obviously prefer Devon, who is also a charming man."

"What can I say?" Lara shrugged, still smiling. "Except that I didn't know it showed so clearly."

"Around the edges," Melanie replied with a soft laugh. "Well, good luck."

"Thanks. I may well need it."

Melanie looked at her somewhat curiously, but before she could say anything else their attention was caught by their bellowing director.

"Where the hell's Devon? If the FBI's going to cart him away, for Pete's sake, somebody tell me!"

"Why would they do that?" Devon asked, emerging from the wings looking harassed.

Nick glared at him. "How should I know? Will they?"

"No." Devon glanced around at the curious faces, then sighed and said patiently, "One of my designers at the California branch of Com-Tech had applied for a government job and gave my name as a reference. They're doing a background security check on him, that's all."

"I didn't know the FBI did that," Nick said in his normal voice, interested in spite of himself.

"They do if it's a high-security job," Devon said.

"Oh." Nick visibly shook off the interest. "Well, are you free to rehearse now?"

"Certainly."

"Great. Lara, I want you two to start running your lines together in the tower room."

She hesitated, then said, "Okay, but can I have a couple of minutes first? I'll be right back."

The director rolled his eyes heavenward, and said in a long-suffering voice, "Yeah, sure. Hurry it up, will you?" He clearly thought it was a call of nature.

Lara hurried offstage. She and Devon had decided, after careful thought, that she would have to be fairly obvious in leaving the others soon after the FBI agent had departed, and she had chosen the moment well. Everyone was wandering about as they prepared to get to work for the night, and the absence of anyone who might follow Lara would hardly be noticed.

She went to the heavy stage door and pushed it open about a foot, remaining inside. Immediately, the neatly dressed agent appeared in the opening and flashed his badge.

"Well?" Lara snapped softly.

In a low but perfectly audible voice, the stranger said, "No problem, Miss Callahan. Devon Shane's background checks out completely. He worked at Com-Tech in California for almost ten years and was transferred out here two weeks ago. He's living in a company-leased apartment here in Pinewood and is driving a company car. Aside from one lone unpaid parking ticket, he's clean."

"Should I bet my life on that?" Her voice was even, but held a thread of hostility.

The agent shifted his weight restlessly and said, "Look, I wasn't one of the agents on your case months ago, so don't take it out on me, all right?"

"Sorry." She didn't sound it.

He sighed. "Right. Devon Shane is clean. That was all you wanted to know. Any other problems?"

"No," she said flatly, without hesitating.

"Fine, then. If you get suspicious of anyone or anything again, give us a call. We'll check it out." He waited for an instant, but when she didn't offer any thanks, finished sardonically, "Can I go now?"

"Oh, sure. I wouldn't want you to miss your plane."

With something of a snap, the agent said, "Good-bye, Miss Callahan."

She pulled the door shut, but stood there for a moment without moving. Mentally, she was sending a *Well done!* to the nameless agent who had played his part so well. She was also wondering if this gamble had paid off.

After all they couldn't lead the cartel's man around by a leash; they could only assume that he kept a close watch on her, and that he saw and heard what they wanted him to. If he did, he should now be doubting any suspicions he had concerning Devon.

And he should be aware of the strong implication that Lara's past dealings with the FBI weren't happy ones.

Given all those highly uncertain coulds, shoulds, woulds, mights, and maybes, to say nothing of all the ifs, the cartel's man was right where they wanted him to be.

The ad would run in the Pinewood newspaper tomorrow (Lara had gotten it in just under the deadline), and in the New York and D.C. papers the day after. With a little luck or a benevolent fate (depending on which belief one leaned toward), she and Devon had given the cartel and their man pause.

The cartel would likely be informed by their man that Lara was playing a lone hand. She had used her FBI contacts only to check out the new man in her life while keeping quiet about the definite presence of a hunter, and had simultaneously sent a warning message to the effect that there was still a great deal she could tell the FBI, if she wanted to do so.

The message, which she and Devon had worded very carefully, was imprinted on her mind. To an unaware reader, it would seem like a simple, if somewhat obscure, personal ad; but to those who understood, it may as well have glowed in neon.

To Whom It May Concern: Lara Mason wishes to thank those interested in her welfare after the death of her father. At present, she has no intention of continuing the late Dr. Mason's work herself, but assures interested parties that said work did not die with him. She asks that anyone concerned contact her for further details.

Following was a post office box number, which

neither Lara nor Devon expected anyone to make use of.

Mason, the name Lara had been born with, stood out boldly in the ad, along with her father's. It would catch the eye—certainly the eye of a watcher who was looking for just such an ad.

"Lara!"

She shook off the thoughts and headed back toward the stage, forcing all signs of tension from her face. She wanted to present the appearance of a woman who had been reassured somewhat during the brief trip offstage, but who was still troubled by other fears. A woman who was hiding those troubling thoughts, not from a possible assassin, but from the new man in her life.

She didn't know how well she carried it off. There was no opportunity to talk privately with Devon for quite some time, since Nick immediately placed them in the tower room set and had them begin running lines.

Surprisingly, considering all the tensions inside her, Lara found it easy to rehearse the careful, gently tentative first scene with Rapunzel and her prince together in the tower. Though her love for Devon had ended her isolation, she remembered only too well how it felt, and had no difficulty in recreating in her voice and expression that scared aloneness, the wistfulness of being apart from others.

Nick, who was sitting just beyond the set and observing them closely, seemed more than satisfied. "Good," he murmured from time to time. He became so involved with their portrayals, in fact, that he skipped the scene of the witch's return to the tower and asked them to continue their scenes alone together.

"I want a sense of continuity," he explained, his expression intense. "Make sure the developing relationship works. And follow the stage directions, please; I want to see how well you two move together."

Lara was vaguely aware that the work on stage had halted, and that cast and crew alike were watching silently from various points on the stage, but she didn't really notice. Nick had ordered the tower room spotlighted, leaving the remainder of the stage in shadows.

They were virtually in a world of their own, surrounded by stone walls and darkness. The tower room was draped with bright, colorful silk hangings, and the furniture was dressed up to look opulent. There was a wide bed with tall posts topped with a canopy, a battered piano with a splash of gilded paint here and there as evidence that it was in the process of being converted into something much grander, a dressing table without a mirror, curved walls without a door.

There was a narrow, plush couch strewn with colorful, tasseled pillows like those on the bed, and that was where Nick's stage direction placed the lovers. Ching, uninvited at the moment but nonetheless in his assigned position, had leapt onto the bed and watched silently.

Devon and Lara hadn't memorized their lines yet, but since they had been rehearsing only a few days, Nick hadn't expected them to. They held their scripts and read the lines, following the stage directions closely—at least at first.

But as the scene progressed, Lara forgot that she was obeying instructions to move this way or that. The emotions Nick had written into his play were so intense, and so intensely felt by her, that the actions flowed naturally from that wellspring of deep feeling. The prince with Devon's haunting voice and bottomless eyes held her captive more surely than any stone tower could have done.

And that was no prison.

Her longing for him was her own, shining through Rapunzel's innocent trust; her desire glowed in her eyes and in the shy expression of Rapunzel; her love was a husky, wordless need in Rapunzel's sweet voice.

Devon knew that the intensity between them now would never be reproduced on a stage before an audience. Because it wasn't a play they were performing. Though their director couldn't know it, what he was seeing was a fervor born of an awareness he would likely never understand.

They had staked everything on a gamble that risked their very lives, and now they shared the knowledge that they were committed . . . and that they could lose.

The first kiss between Rapunzel and her prince was infinitely tender, yet beneath the gentleness was the raging of a storm trapped under glass. And on each succeeding visit by the prince, with each touch, that storm grew wilder and wilder, until it could no longer be contained.

"Hold it! Lights!"

The abrupt interruption should have been jarring, but it wasn't. Somehow, in that intense awareness between them, both Lara and Devon had found something that insulated them and left them incredibly alive as only those who have faced their own mortality can be.

The prince had lifted Rapunzel into his arms and taken a step toward the bed, and now Devon lowered Lara gently to her feet and spoke to the director with utter calm.

"Ching's embarrassed, Nick. You didn't tell him when he was supposed to give up the bed to us."

"Yah!" Ching said, sending the director an annoyed glare.

"Never embarrass a cat," Lara murmured, wondering vaguely what she had done with her script. And what Devon had done with his. "You won't be forgiven for it quickly."

Nick gave the cat a somewhat blank look, then drew a shaken breath and said, "Lord, you two won't bring the house down—you'll *burn* it down!"

Lara sat on the bed and reached to pet her cat. "You wrote the play, Nick," she reminded him with a tranquil calm that matched Devon's.

"I didn't write what I just saw—and felt. Nobody could write that." Somewhat wistfully, he added, "I'd give ten years of my life if I could, though."

"Never wish your life away," Lara said in a light tone. She didn't look at Devon because that glance would have betrayed them both.

Much later, Lara snuggled closer to Devon and smiled as his arms tightened around her. They were in her bed, alone together in the darkness. Outside, his men used all their professional experience to make certain their close observation of the building went unnoticed by another watcher. Ching, still embarrassed about his missing cue, since he shared the feline trait of having a high opinion of his own dignity, had finally given up his muttering and sulk-ing, and had gone to sleep in the living room.

"Think we pulled it off?" she murmured.

"I don't know," Devon said quietly. "You were cer-tainly convincing."

"Who left the stage after I did?"

He sighed. "I lost sight of most of them at one time or another."

"Luke?"

"Yes."

"Who *didn't* leave the stage?"

"Nick. I don't think Sonia did, but I'm not sure."

It was Lara's turn to sigh. "And we can't be cer-tain that the bait was taken at all. It could be any of them, couldn't it?"

"Realistically, yes. But in fairness to them, it could also be someone neither of us has seen."

"I'd rather it were that."

Devon rubbed his cheek gently against her soft hair. "I know. But, until we're sure . . ."

She was silent for a moment, but very much awake. "Why did you become an agent?"

"I don't think it was ever a conscious choice. I was recruited out of college, and even though I had a law degree, I hadn't really decided what to do with it."

"No desire to be an attorney?"

"There are too many in this country now. I stud-ied law just because it interested me. When the bureau made me an offer, I decided to try it."

"Regrets?"

"No, not for that decision." He hesitated, then went on quietly. "I was on the brink of quitting when I was given this assignment."

"Why?" she asked softly.

"I was beginning to lose myself. There was one role after another, and the line between right and wrong was harder and harder to see. Sometimes I've looked at someone I had deliberately gotten close to and then betrayed, and I haven't known who was worse—my enemy or me."

Lara listened to his haunting voice and knew now where his pain came from. It was a pain she could only dimly understand, but it explained the struggle she had felt in him from the beginning.

She lifted her head from his chest and gazed at him. Even in the darkness of the bedroom, his eyes were vivid. Softly, she said, "You once said to me that platitudes couldn't ease pain. You were right, and I won't offer them. But, Devon, if you were as bad as your enemies, or worse than them, betrayal would be easy. It wouldn't hurt."

He slid a hand under the warm weight of her hair and kissed her gently, then guided her back to her resting place. "I hope you're right," he murmured almost inaudibly.

Eight

"His background checks out," the voice on the other end of the line said flatly.

"What about the other one?"

"Clean too. You must have been jumping at shadows. From what you heard, it looks like the girl hates the feds and hasn't told them she thinks someone's after her. The bit with Shane was apparently just common sense; they're in bed together, so she wanted him checked out. But the feds don't know we've found her."

"Sure about that?"

"Aren't you?"

"I don't know. Maybe they were rough on her when her father died. Maybe she's got no love for them. And maybe she figures the constant presence of the boyfriend will keep her safe, at least for a few days."

"A few days?" The voice at the other end of the line sharpened.

"Yeah. She needs at least a few days to be certain we've gotten the message."

"What message?"

"It's in today's Pinewood newspaper. A classified ad." The caller didn't read from the newspaper folded on the ledge beneath the phone, even though the bright morning light would have made it easy. Instead, Lara's message was recited coolly from memory.

There was a long silence.

The caller waited patiently for a few moments, then said, "It begins to look as if we've all missed something."

"You're sure her apartment was clean?"

"Of course. I could have missed a piece of microfilm, I suppose, but nothing else, and her father hardly had the time to get that fancy. Look, she was in shock when the FBI took her into protective custody; they let her pack a small bag, and you can bet an agent was standing over her when she did. She didn't take anything out of there that night, and she hasn't been back to the house."

Slowly, the caller said, "A bluff?"

"Could be. And it could be that either she's remembered something about that night or else she knew where the evidence was all along."

"Then why keep quiet about it?" The caller caught his breath suddenly. "Blackmail?"

"She's bright enough to think of it. She's also bright enough to figure out that she's fairly safe as long as we know the evidence could be used against us. I don't think she's the blackmail type. But if that conversation with the agent was genuine, she might well prefer to deal with us rather than with them."

The caller thought that over. "But does she have the evidence?"

"You told me that your people had to search the house quickly; maybe they missed it."

"The FBI searched, and they had the time to do it right."

"It's still possible they missed it. You told me that you had reason to believe she was more of a threat than was originally thought. Why?"

The caller hesitated, then said briefly, "Shortly after Dr.—shortly after her father's death, we discovered a number of items missing. The trail strongly indicated that her father had taken them; he had the means to blow our organization to splinters. The FBI wouldn't have hesitated to use that immediately, if they had found it."

"So you were certain the evidence did exist. And certain she was a possible threat from the beginning. Why was I told only after I arrived here?"

"Even then, there was a remote possibility that the viper was in our own house. However, we're now certain that only the doctor could have gotten the evidence. And the only remaining link to the doctor is his daughter."

"I see. Well, do I go after her, or wait and let her lead me to the evidence?"

"Do you think she will?"

"I think that if she does know where it is, she also knows it's no damn good to her. It might be in the house. Or her father may have hidden at least part of it somewhere else and told her where. In any case, as you said, she's the only link. Unless she protects herself by getting the evidence to someone who'll use it if anything happens to her, she's running a colossal bluff. She has to protect herself."

After a moment, the caller said, "So she warns us that the evidence exists, hoping we'll back off long enough for her to make the bluff real."

"It would be the smart move. She gives us a couple of days to get the message, then shakes the boyfriend, slips out, and goes after the evidence while we're deciding what to do about her."

"Amateur."

"Of course. But not a fool."

"There's no sign she's under FBI surveillance?"

"Not that I've been able to find. There's no tap on her phone, no vehicles parked suspiciously close to her building, no unscheduled work being done in the area. The agent who came in last night caught a plane back to D.C. as soon as he'd talked to her."

"What about her car?"

"Still at the theater. She's been riding with Shane, and may not know it's been tampered with."

"If she does go after the evidence, what about her car?"

"I don't think she'll drive her own car; she knows she's being watched; that's obvious. If I were in her place, I'd take a bus, then hire a car in D.C. Safer."

"*If* she goes back to the house."

"Right."

"Would she assume someone was following her?"

"Certainly. And probably lead me on a wild goose chase in D.C. in order to lose me. Most amateurs believe a tail isn't that hard to lose."

"She'd feel safe?"

"I'd make sure of it."

The caller said, "Hold on," and there was a soft hiss of static on the line for a few moments. When he came back on, it was clear there had been a discussion. "Keep an eye on her. A very close eye. We'll give her a few days."

"You want the evidence?"

"Yes. If she leaves Pinewood, don't lose her."

"And if she leads me to the evidence?"

"Get it. Then kill her."

"It won't do any good," Lara said flatly. "I can't remember anything else about that night, because I didn't see or hear anything."

Devon watched her moving restlessly around the living room of her apartment. It was early on Saturday, and both would be expected at the theater within a few hours to rehearse. He knew Lara was tense, jittery because they could only wait blindly with no certainty that their plan would work; he was tense himself, and he had much more experience than she at this sort of thing.

But he was still convinced that Lara knew more than she realized, and he wanted that knowledge desperately. If he could only get the evidence into his hands, he could stop this madness without risking Lara's life.

"We can try," he said now, quietly.

"I'm not ready."

Devon hesitated, and only his determination to keep her safe made him press her. "Honey, you're never going to be ready. No one is ever ready to face something like this. But you have to try."

"It hurts! Don't you understand?"

"Yes," he said. "I understand.'

Lara looked at him, and her tense face softened. "I know. I know you do."

"Then you know I wouldn't ask you to do this if I didn't believe it could help us."

After a moment, she went to the couch and sat

down beside him. "All right," she said steadily. "If you really think so, I'll try."

Devon took one of her hands in his, holding it firmly. "Close your eyes," he instructed, and when she obeyed, he went on in a soft voice, "I want you to think about returning to your house that night. Imagine every step, see everything you saw that night. Start at the beginning. Were you driving yourself?"

"No. Some friends drove me home. They let me out in front of the house. At the sidewalk." Lara was determined to really try, because Devon wanted her to. So she concentrated intently. "It was chilly, so I hurried to the front door."

"Was the house dark?"

"Yes. But that isn't unusual. There's a redwood fence, so you can only see the front windows. Dad's study is on the side, and he never remembers to leave the porch light on. Or the foyer light." She was unconscious of having shifted to the present tense, and Devon held her there so smoothly that she didn't notice it.

"You have your key?"

"Yes. I unlock the door and go in. As soon as I shut it behind me. I reach for the light switch. Ching howls. He—he sounds funny. I've never heard him sound like that."

Devon glanced at the cat, who was sprawled on his side under the coffee table and snoring almost inaudibly. "Do you think something's wrong with him?" he asked her.

"No. He sounds angry. Afraid."

"All right. Turn the light on. What do you see?"

"The foyer. Someone's knocked the magazines and newspapers off the table. It's a mess." A frown flitted suddenly across her still face.

"What are you looking at?" Devon asked softly, watching her face.

"Ching. He's at the top of the stairs. Upset. I don't think he wants to come down. The house is very quiet. I feel cold. I call out for Dad, but he doesn't answer. I walk across the foyer and knock on his study door."

"Do you hear anything from inside?"

"No. But Dad gets so deeply involved in his work that he often doesn't answer. So it's still all right."

Devon felt a pang of hurt for her. She'd already guessed something was wrong, maybe even knew what she'd find when she opened the door; it was in her voice. But she was trying to convince herself that nothing was wrong. He wished he didn't have to ask this of her.

But he had no choice. "Open the door," he told her gently.

"I don't want to," she whispered.

"I know. But you have to. Open the door."

Lara caught her breath. "Oh, dear God . . ."

The hand he was holding was cold, the fingers tightening almost convulsively around his. "Look at the room, Lara," he ordered firmly. "Just the room. Tell me what you see. Start at the door, and look clockwise around the room."

Her breathing was shallow, and her voice emerged so strained, it was little more than a whisper. "There's a chair by the door; the cushions have been ripped and torn. There are books scattered on the floor. Dad's reading lamp is lying on its side with the shade gone. Just past that is the big prayer plant, uprooted from its pot." A quiver disturbed her face. "'Dad likes plants."

"Keep looking, Lara," Devon told her gently. "What else do you see?"

"The window. The drapes have been ripped down and—and shredded. Why would someone do that?"

"I don't know."

"There was too much to hide in the drapes," she murmured in a puzzled tone. "Dad said it was a lot. Diagrams and photographs, and all the computer records."

Devon almost held his breath. "That sounds like a lot."

"Yes. And he had something with fingerprints. He wouldn't tell me what it was, but he said it was safe. He said it would hold up in court." She fell silent.

After a moment, Devon prompted softly, "Did he say anything else?"

"Hmmm? Oh. No, he wouldn't tell me. He said not to worry. But I did."

"All right. Now tell me about the room. You were looking at the window."

"Bookshelves with all the books pulled out. Another window; those drapes are torn down too. There was a table in front of it; it's all smashed, and the vase that was on it is broken on the floor. Then more shelves and—Dad's desk. I can see his computer; it's on, but there's nothing on the screen. I think someone's wiped everything off the hard disk, even the operating system; the machine's just humming."

"Are there any diskettes?" Devon asked. The FBI agents had found none.

"Floppies? No. They must have taken them. Dad always kept the hard disk backed up on floppies. There was a file case for them, but I don't see it anywhere."

"All right. What do you see?"

"They've been into his safe. It's behind the desk, very obvious behind a painting. I told Dad it was obvious, but he said that was okay, he never kept anything important in there. They've ripped the painting and broken the hinges."

"Look at the desk, Lara. Look carefully."

"I see it. There's nothing. Just the computer. The papers and files that are usually there are on the floor, mostly torn in pieces."

"Fine. Now keep looking clockwise around the room."

She drew a shuddering breath. "Dad's on the floor. He looks—"

"Easy, honey. Easy. Look at it as if it's a picture. Just a photograph."

"But it isn't. It's real. They've killed him . . ." Her voice wavered, unsteady with horror and pain. Abruptly, her eyes snapped open, blind for an instant. "I can't. I can't keep looking—"

Devon pulled her into his arms and held her tightly, stroking her soft hair. "All right. All right, honey. You did just fine. Don't think about it anymore."

For a moment, Lara held on to him, but then she pushed back far enough to meet his concerned gaze. "It doesn't matter," she said tiredly. "There wasn't anything else. Dad's desk was to the right of the door. I told you I wouldn't think of anything to help us."

He was silent, his arms still around her. Then, quietly, he said, "You told me more than you told the agents who questioned you before."

"I did?" She was puzzled. "What?"

"That your father had something with fingerprints."

Lara thought about it, but shook her head. "I don't see that it helps us."

"It tells us that your father's evidence wasn't something that could have been wiped off a computer disk. And that it was evidence he believed to be safe. He hid it somewhere, Lara. The cartel didn't find it, and we didn't find it. So it still exists."

"Somewhere."

"Yes. Somewhere."

"I don't know where it is."

Devon hesitated, then said, "I can't believe he'd hide it so thoroughly that professionals couldn't find it without making sure you could. He was in danger, and he knew it; there was every possibility that the cartel might guess what he was up to and stop him. He had to protect you."

Lara shook her head. "You know what he told me. Nothing. Just that he had evidence that would stand up in court. Devon, he never told me where it was. I've gone over every conversation of those last few days; he just said that the less I knew, the better it would be."

Devon was silent.

She managed a faint smile. "So there won't be a last-minute reprieve."

"Don't say that," he told her instantly. "Don't say it as if—"

"As if I've been condemned?"

"Dammit, Lara."

"Hey, I haven't given up yet. We have a chance of catching the cartel's man, and maybe that'll be enough."

Devon held her a bit tighter, unwilling to tell her that he doubted it would be. The cartel's man was likely to be a professional hired for this job, with little or no knowledge of the men he was working for. Even if he turned out to be a totally cooperative witness, the chances were good that he would be able to tell them nothing that would help.

Lara would still be a threat to the cartel.

And another killer would be sent after her.

He didn't want to tell her any of that, and tried to keep his own cold awareness from showing on his face. But it seemed that either he wasn't the natural actor he was supposed to be, or else the tie with Lara simply made it impossible for him to hide from her any emotion as deep and strong as his fear.

"It's all right, Devon," she said gently.

He kissed her, needing that, then murmured, "Is it?"

"All I hope to gain from the bluff is a little more time. I know it isn't a solution."

She knew; he didn't have to tell her anything. His throat was so tight, he could hardly speak. "It'll do one thing, if we catch their man. They'll lose track of you, at least for a while."

Lara waited, watching his face gravely.

"We can . . . hide you again."

"It's still my choice," she said.

"Yes." That battle had already been fought; he understood pain and loneliness too well not to accept that it was her decision, her right to choose.

"Another apartment, another town, another name—another life with no roots. Another prison."

He had expected an instant refusal of that option, but wasn't sure from her toneless voice how she felt about it. He held his own voice steady. "Lara, you can't run a bluff indefinitely. There's an outside chance that a good legal case can be built against the cartel's man. In that case we could give him and his associates enough heat to keep them busy for a while. But it's more likely that he won't know anything about them, and won't be much use to us in going after them."

"So they'll send someone else after me."

"Yes. We'll have to get you away, honey."

Lara pulled away from him. She didn't pace, but moved around the room almost as if she'd never really looked at it before. Finally, she began musing aloud, her voice soft and faraway. "You know, I always thought that Rapunzel and her prince complicated the problem needlessly. All that stuff about a silken cord being woven into a ladder, when the solution was right in front of them all the time."

She stopped moving and faced him. "All she had to do was cut off the braid, tie it to the window, and climb down. They'd have gotten away free. Why didn't that occur to them?"

"I don't know," Devon said quietly, watching her.

"I think I do." She smiled. "I think it was because of who and what they were. The prince had always had his freedom and didn't value it enough to think of sacrifice; Rapunzel had never known freedom, so she couldn't know it was worth a sacrifice."

"You'd cut off your hair."

"Yes. But that isn't my problem."

Devon got up and went to her, feeling a tug that reminded him of that other time and the pain of raw emotions. He wasn't going to like the answer, he knew that, but he had to ask anyway. "Then what is?"

"I love you, Devon."

His heart seemed to stop, and then pound erratically inside his chest. He managed a smile. "That's a problem?"

"Inside a tower it is." She stared up at him with steady, somber eyes. "Because I think that you believe what I feel wouldn't survive outside that tower. If I let you take me somewhere safe, to another tower, you'll never be sure, will you? You'll always wonder if, like Rapunzel, I fell for the first prince who climbed in the window."

"Lara—"

"Oh, I know we haven't talked about a future. We haven't been able to. But if it's just good sex as far as you're concerned, I wish you'd tell me now, because—"

"No." His hands found her shoulders, and he gave her a little shake without really being aware of it. "No, dammit. I want you in my life."

The tie between them, she thought dimly. Blessing or burden; it seemed Devon still wasn't sure. But at least he was unwilling to lose it, and that was something. She took a deep breath. "Then I have to cut off the braid."

He knew what she was saying. Unlike Rapunzel and her prince, Lara knew freedom was worth a sacrifice, and she was willing to make it. But she could lose more than a beautiful golden braid; she could lose her life.

"I want you safe," he said huskily. "Nothing is as important as that."

"One thing is. I love you, Devon. That won't change, inside a tower or out. But you don't believe it. I could live in a prison with you and never notice the bars. But I could never live with your doubt. Until I'm free to walk away, you'll always wonder if I would."

He couldn't lie to her, and he knew it; the emotional bond between them was too strong to allow for a deception. He couldn't persuade her that what she believed was wrong, because it wasn't. Even with a soul-deep desire to trust that a love born in captivity could survive freedom, he couldn't believe it.

"Lara—"

She lifted a hand, her fingers lightly covering his lips. "It's all right, Devon. I've known it all along. But some things are worth risking everything for. It's my choice." Smiling, she slipped her arms around his neck. "Now, since we have a couple of hours before we have to be at the theater to rehearse . . ."

The rehearsals on Saturday went as planned, with nothing unexpected occurring. It was the same on Sunday. Devon stuck close to Lara, and neither of them made any effort to hide their relationship offstage. The entire cast and crew was rapidly aware that Rapunzel had indeed found her prince, and Nick got rather sentimental about it.

Lara practiced the *Moonlight* Sonata on an old piano that boasted more gilded paint with every day that passed and that, at one point, sprouted a few colorful feathers owing to the playful taste of one of the crew. They went over lines and marks, and were fitted for costumes. Devon was talked out of a minor rebellion when he saw the tights intended for him, but only after a compromise of boots and knee-breeches was reached. Ching was given his cues by Nick, who knew and understood cats. Ching performed like a trouper. The scenery began to take shape, and the crew practiced the set changes under the frowning eye of a director with a stopwatch.

Inside the theater, the play began to come together, and since it was the weekend, everyone spent most of both days working at it.

Nothing unusual happened. Lara rode in Devon's car and more or less ignored her own. Luke was friendly, but didn't go overboard on the charm, and if he still had doubts about Devon, he kept them to himself. He tried twice more to seduce Ching with first chicken, then tuna; but since the cat had progressed from open hostility to cold disdain, he didn't get very far.

On Sunday night, at midnight, a bus was due to pass through town on its way to Washington. Lara planned to be on it. She and Devon had talked it over, and their plans were carefully laid. Since he had been spending every night at her apartment, Devon thought it would look too suspicious for him to leave on this night; and since the lights in the apartment went out well before midnight, the watcher outside could speculate that Devon was, on this night, sleeping the sleep of the just. And the weary.

The simplest explanation is usually the most believed.

Lara would creep out in darkness, presumably leaving her lover a note, and walk to the bus depot just a few short blocks of lighted streets away. Two agents, strategically placed well beforehand, would make certain she reached her destination. Devon would wait in the apartment for an hour, at which time he'd be relieved by a third agent, who would take his place on the chance that the watcher would decide to check on Devon's presence.

Then, Devon would slip out the back to a waiting car, drive to a private airfield, and take a waiting helicopter directly to Washington. He didn't want to let Lara out of his sight at all, and took small comfort from the fact that an agent would be aboard the bus when it entered and left Pinewood, and that she would be very discreetly escorted all the way to her father's house.

Lara had been impressed by the number of agents involved in the plan, but had to admit that if her father's beliefs had been correct, any effort to stop the cartel would be worthwhile.

She felt as protected as was possible under the circumstances and didn't hesitate to tell Devon so. She was afraid, of course. She would have had to be an idiot not to be conscious of fear. But she was committed, certain of her reasons for that commitment, and very conscious of the knowledge that doing something was better than doing nothing.

So, near midnight on Sunday, she was able to draw about her a cloak of calm resolve and say goodbye to Devon without shattering into a million pieces.

"I'll see you at the house," he said, resisting the finality of a good-bye and pulling her close in a fierce embrace at the door.

It was dark; she couldn't see his face clearly. She returned his kiss with all the feeling inside her, then murmured, "I love you," and left while she still could.

Devon was alone in a dark, silent apartment. Almost alone. Though not noticeably nocturnal, as most cats are, Ching was very much awake now, and restless. He prowled about, murmuring to himself and occasionally uttering a soft comment to

Devon. He didn't want to be held or petted, and it was obvious that his idol's tension was affecting him.

It was the longest hour of Devon's life. He could no more be still than the cat could, and he wandered around the dark apartment filled with such a storm of emotions, it was like being battered by something he couldn't see. He felt that he had failed Lara at a desperately critical moment, and the pain and self-disgust of that was killing him.

God, why hadn't he told her he loved her? He did. He'd known it for days. Why hadn't he been able to say it? Just three simple words. . . . And it was his fault she was out there now, his fault she was risk-ing everything. Him and his selfish doubts. Had the last ten years made him such a coward that he'd allow her to risk her very life in order to spare him the pain of uncertainty?

I could live in a prison with you and never no-tice the bars.

It was true, and he knew it. Without his doubts standing between them, Lara would have been will-ing to be hidden again, given a new name and iden-tity, because she wouldn't have been alone and could have built a new, strong life for herself. But that kind of quiet sacrifice had to be sustained by trust, and how could she trust a man who had no belief in the reality of her love?

Devon stopped pacing abruptly and stared blindly at nothing.

All that stuff about a silken cord being woven into a ladder, when the solution was right in front of them all the time.

What was he most afraid of? Until tonight, he had

been afraid to trust in Lara's love because ten years of roles had left him flinching away from any risk of pain. But he was hurting now, and he knew why.

It wasn't the risk that brought pain, he realized. It was the unwillingness to risk. That was why he'd been tearing himself apart. He hadn't been willing to risk anything with Lara. Get her away safe, yes—but she'd be in a prison, and he couldn't risk that. Love her, yes—but don't tell her, because that made him vulnerable, and heaven knew he couldn't risk that. Let her choose to be bait for a dangerous trap, yes—because he couldn't choose, couldn't risk being wrong, terribly wrong.

And a tower was only a prison when you weren't willing to cut off the damned braid and get the hell out.

In that instant of realization, Devon made a choice of his own. He glanced at his watch and knew that his agent would be there at any moment. Swiftly, he went down the hall and into Lara's bedroom, and got the cat carrier out of the closet.

Before a surprised Ching could struggle, the cat found himself stuffed into the box. And the first note of his enraged howl was cut off by his idol's soft but utterly implacable command.

"Quiet! Or you'll ride in the trunk."

Ching shut up.

Two minutes later, Devon opened the door to allow his agent to slip in.

"Well?" he demanded.

"It's a go. A car fell in behind the bus as it left town. And if anybody's watching this building, I'll turn in my pension."

"For both our sakes, I hope you don't have to.

Thanks, Mac. Stay here just to be sure. I'm taking the cat."

"Thought I was supposed to cat-sit?"

"You were. But I've got a hunch."

"It's your party. Call me when the shouting's over."

"Right." Devon, with a tough plastic box containing a silent but mutinous cat in hand, slipped out of the apartment. In minutes, he went out the back and found his car and driver waiting with lights off and quiet engine running. He put the carrier in the backseat and got in.

"Hurry," he ordered.

Lara had expected memories to overwhelm her, but when she stepped into the foyer and turned on the lights, it was almost like entering a totally strange house. It was clean; a service came in monthly to dust and vacuum. The electricity was still on because she had refused to allow it to be turned off. It was quiet because it was supposed to be empty.

She wanted to walk through the house, to find some sense of familiarity, but she knew time was short. The car she had "rented" at the bus depot had been equipped with a very special radio, and an agent had informed her that her hunter was very close on her heels.

Taking a deep breath, she crossed the foyer and went into her father's study. It was neat again, the books on their shelves, torn drapes and upholstery replaced, the desk tidy. As if nothing had happened here.

Lara went to the desk and sat down, keeping her mind occupied with what she had to do. Take the diskette from the pocket of her jacket and put it in the computer disk drive. Turn on the machine. Wait for it to load the program into its memory.

She knew Devon was here; she could feel his presence. There were others here as well, hidden in the house. The place was wired. The trap was set, and baited.

She looked at the waiting computer, then began keying in commands. Lines of data began racing across the glowing screen.

"Hello, Lara."

She looked up and, after an instant of total surprise, decided that it made perfect sense. "Oh," she said slowly. She kept her fingers on the keyboard, but didn't move them. "I should have paid attention to Ching."

"Yes." Melanie said gently, coming into the room. "You should have."

She was holding an automatic equipped with a silencer.

Nine

"And I should have paid more attention to the play," Lara said. "There were so many similarities. I should have suspected the witch."

"Who did you suspect?" Melanie asked, halting a couple of feet back from the desk. "Luke? Or was Devon the one you were worried about, especially after he got into your bed?"

"Luke. I never thought of you."

Melanie studied her, dark eyes as hard as chips of coal. "Why didn't you have him checked out the way you did Devon?"

"It didn't matter who it was, as long as it wasn't Devon. And I didn't want the bureau getting jumpy because I pushed the panic button twice in one week." Lara allowed her voice to sound a bit grim on the last statement.

Lifting one delicately arched brow, Melanie said, "Makes sense. So you did want to play a lone hand."

"You got my message?"

"Certainly. It sounded suspiciously like blackmail."

"I just want to be left alone," Lara said.

"Or?" Melanie smiled tauntingly. "Never pick up a big stick unless you're prepared to use it, sweetie."

Lara suddenly pressed the return key, and the click was loud in the silence. The computer hummed busily. "I just used it," she said softly.

The dark woman's eyes narrowed, and she went very still. Her gun was trained steadily on the center of Lara's chest. "What have you done?" she snapped.

"Know anything about computers?"

"I know the memory of that one was wiped."

In a reflective tone, Lara said, "It's damnably easy to accidentally destroy computer data. Just press a few keys, and it's gone. Dad was an expert; he always backed up his data. I know you people took the diskettes, but I also know you found nothing of use on them."

"Get to the point," Melanie ordered.

"Gladly. Dad developed a special code purely for his own use. Once he had it perfected, it was possible to hide data on the hard disk so completely that even a total crash of the system wouldn't touch it. The hidden data could be destroyed only if the hard disk was physically destroyed—or with a special code that only he knew. But he gave me the retrieval code."

Melanie's gaze flicked briefly to the computer; from her position, she could see only a blank, glowing screen. The screen was set at an angle, but the keyboard was set squarely on the blotter so that Lara was facing forward. "Where is it? Where's the data?"

"I sent it away," Lara said.

Stiffening, Melanie glanced quickly over the bare desk. It held the computer, a blotter, and a telephone. Nothing else. "You couldn't have. There's no modem."

Lara let herself smile, but took care not to make it too triumphant. "This machine has an internal modem, hooked directly into the phone line."

Melanie took half a step and, keeping the gun pointed at Lara, lifted the receiver. She didn't even have to hold it to her ear; they could both hear the tones of a busy computer coming through the phone line. She slammed the receiver back into place and stared at Lara.

For one awful, endless instant, Lara thought that the woman would just take the chance and shoot her. But then Melanie seemed to relax very slightly.

"Where did you send it?" she asked casually.

"Do you seriously expect me to answer that?"

"Oh, just generally, I mean." Melanie smiled.

Lara shrugged. "Why not? Dad had friends all over the country, most with computers. A group of them made an agreement years ago that they would each leave at least one system on-line at all times. To exchange messages and so on."

Melanie's eyes narrowed again. "What makes you so sure the system you chose is still active?"

"Well, I didn't really want to take that chance. But I do believe that at least *one* of the three I chose will be." She heard the soft curse from the other woman, and kept her own gaze steady and calm. "It's almost dawn here; what with the various time zones, I doubt any of the gentlemen are awake right now. But when they check their systems, they'll find a big, bright message flag, along with a sizable chunk of data. I believe you know the gist of the data. The message is 'Read immediately, print out a hard copy of all data, and then convey it to the FBI.' "

Lara waited for a long moment, then said quietly, "Unless, of course, I alter that message."

"What do you want?" Melanie asked flatly.

"Who killed my father?"

"You won't get that answer."

"I think that depends. I think it depends on how badly the organization you work for wants to avoid its day in court. Are you authorized to make that decision? Or shall we hold this stalemate until the question becomes academic? It's your move, Melanie."

"How much time do I have?"

"At a guess less than an hour before the message is received by at least one of those men. After that, it's out of my hands."

"And you'll be dead."

Lara didn't let her surprise show; she hadn't expected the other woman to admit that. "Maybe," she said. "But it seems stupid to me. The FBI doesn't need me to testify once they have the data, and you'd have a hell of a time collecting your pay from employers scrambling to stay out of jail."

"You could testify against *me*, though. I really wouldn't want that."

"Testify against you for what? Holding a gun on me? My word against yours. I can't prove you've done anything to me at all." Lara knew her time was running out. She had already kept Melanie talking longer than she'd expected to. But what she was hoping for with everything inside her was that the woman would place a call to her employers. Any call going out from this phone would be immediately traced. Sort of. According to Devon, one of the bureau's newest gadgets enabled it to pinpoint the location of an outgoing call within twenty seconds flat.

The call would be recorded, of course, even as agents descended on the receiving phone. It was their one slim hope of connecting this paid assassin with those who had hired her. The location could well be a disused storefront, and Melanie's contact a buffer between her and her employers—but it was a chance.

"All right, what do you want?" Melanie asked briskly. "Reasonable demands, if you don't mind."

"I do mind. But I'm not a fool. I have only one demand. I want to be left alone, totally and completely."

"We have to know you're not bluffing."

"I assumed that. If your employers can access a computer, I can send them an edited copy of the data."

"Edited?"

"Certainly. I won't give up all my aces."

Melanie grimaced slightly, but there was more respect than annoyance in the expression. She nodded.

Calmly, Lara said, "In case you're wondering, I'm keeping my fingers on these keys in order to send an end code to the systems holding the data. Notice that I have one finger on the shift."

"Don't tell me. A dead man's switch?"

Afraid so. If I release the shift without first entering a rather complicated code, my earlier message is locked into the systems that received it. And this system will shut itself down. You wouldn't have a hope in hell of recovering the data. But if you want to use that phone, I can switch this computer onto a secondary line. Your move."

"Do it," Melanie said, somewhat irritably.

Leaving one finger of her left hand on the shift key, Lara used her right fingers to tap out a rapid command. When Melanie lifted the phone's receiver, they could both hear a dial tone.

The dark woman kept the gun on Lara and punched out a number quickly.

Lara felt a wave of weariness wash over her and tried to fight it. Almost over now, she told herself. Twenty seconds or so for the call to be pinpointed, and then everyone would be getting ready. They'd wait as long as possible in the hope that either Melanie or her contact would say something incriminating through a careless statement or two—but they couldn't afford to wait long. The moment Melanie's employers demanded that the "evidence" be sent to them, the bluff was lost.

There was a great deal of very carefully selected information on the diskette Lara was using, since it had been especially written for this particular bluff. But there was absolutely nothing that the cartel would have found threatening.

Lara glanced at her watch and waited until thirty seconds had passed, just to be sure. Then she looked at Melanie, although she heard not one word the other woman was saying. There seemed to be a roaring in her ears, and everything was moving so slowly. Even Melanie's mouth. It was terrifyingly fascinating. Seconds crawled by. And then Melanie took the phone away from her ear and started to say something to Lara.

Lara couldn't look away from Melanie, even though

she was dimly aware of movement behind her. She knew that it should be over, and without fuss, any minute now. Melanie was a pro, after all; she wouldn't kill somebody in full view of half a dozen federal agents. They were counting on that.

They hadn't counted on a nervous assassin.

Melanie looked startled—still in slow motion as far as Lara was concerned—and began to turn toward the door. Her gun went off. Lara barely heard the hollow, whistling pop. But she definitely felt the sledgehammer that slammed into her chest, or maybe it was her shoulder, but she was going over backward awfully hard. . . .

"Calm down, Devon! She bumped her head, that's all. Okay, she'll have a bruise, but nothing was broken! Stop trying to wake her up, she probably needs the sleep. And go let the cat out of his box, will you? The neighbors will think we're murdering somebody over here. . . ."

Lara was very tired. She thought about waking up, because she knew somebody wanted her to, but it was too much effort. She felt safe and loved and warm. It felt wonderfully good, so she just kept sleeping. At least until a demand she'd been trained not to ignore forced its way into the depths of her peaceful dreams.

"Wauur?"

"No," she mumbled. "I'm tired."

"Yah!"

"Tell Devon. He'll feed you." She had gotten used to saying that during the short time Devon had been virtually living with her, and enjoyed it. She pulled the covers up over her nose. Then Ching rang his bell right next to her ear—and it sounded as if it were inside her aching head.

She gritted her teeth against the stab of agony. "Oh! Go away, you furry menace. . . ."

Ching muttered.

"I know," Devon said sympathetically, "she really can be infernally stubborn, can't she?"

Lara was about to go back to sleep, but when he spoke she suddenly remembered what had happened. At least up to a point. After that, she was blank. She fumbled the covers down, and would have sat up instantly except that she was afraid she'd leave her head behind on the pillow. Instead, she very cautiously opened her eyes.

Aqua eyes in a striped, furry face stared down at her. They looked annoyed. She turned her head carefully to check out the other side of the bed, and found Devon sitting on the edge gazing down at her.

"Hello," he said.

Lara thought about what her first remark to him should be. She decided to say something wonderfully loving and romantic; this was a moment they should treasure, since she obviously wasn't dead.

"Bulletproof vest, huh!"

"It did stop the bullet," he pointed out politely. Then the faint glimmer of amusement left his eyes, and he added in a totally different voice, "Thank God."

She found the strength to respond when he leaned over and kissed her, but tried to keep what was left of her mind on business. When she could, she asked, "Where's Melanie?"

"In custody."

"And the man she called?"

"Also in custody, and screaming for his lawyer. He was in a nice, respectable broker's office in New York. Early hours to keep for a job like that, but—"

"Dead end?"

"It looks like it. Unless he breaks, we don't have a tie to the cartel."

Lara wasn't really surprised; it had been a slim chance at best. A twinge from her head was echoed by one considerably lower down, and she felt under the covers until she located an extremely sore spot over the center of her rib cage. "Ouch. I feel like I've been kicked by a mule. And what did I hit my head on?"

"The shelf behind the desk."

She probed a bit more, than said, "What am I wearing?"

"A nightgown. I put you into it." Answering the rest of her questions before she could ask them, he said, "It's your nightgown. You're in your own bedroom here at the house, with a couple of agents downstairs. You've been asleep about four hours. One of the men went out for groceries a little while ago, so you'll probably smell burning bacon any minute now. And I love you."

Lara blinked, sifted through the information warily, and found that she still distinctly recalled hearing that last statement. But it seemed odd in the same company as burning bacon. She looked cautiously at Devon, and found him grave and unsmiling.

"Before I make an utter fool of myself," she said slowly, "let me ask you if I just heard what I think I heard."

"I love you," he said.

She felt the pain in her head retreat. It didn't stand a chance. "You love me? Really?"

Devon's grave mask cracked suddenly, and those wonderful eyes glowed with an unshadowed brightness she'd never seen before. "God, *yes*, I love you," he said thickly, gathering her into his arms and holding her.

Lara didn't have to ask if he believed in her own love. She could feel it in him. The affinity between them had never been stronger, and she knew that no tower or prison, with real bars or symbolic ones, would ever isolate either of them again.

"I'm taking a desk job," he announced a few minutes later.

"Do you want that?" she asked, snuggling up to his side in blissful contentment.

"Yes. Make use of that law degree. You are going to marry me, aren't you, Rapunzel?"

"Certainly I am. You don't think I carry on like this with just *any* prince who happens to climb in my window, do you?"

"Well, not if your cat doesn't like him."

"An excellent judge of character, my cat. Do you smell something burning?"

"Bacon. I warned you."

"So you did. I suppose we'd better go rescue it?"

"If we want to eat."

Lara was naturally disappointed that they hadn't managed to get anything on the cartel. She still wanted justice for her father—and she still wanted her own roots back. She had told Devon the truth in saying that she could live in a prison with him and never notice the bars, but it was also undoubtedly true that living with an assumed identity and being aware that a group of powerful people considered you a threat and were actively searching for you did not offer a very good base for a peaceful life.

So when Devon suggested, early that afternoon, that they make one final attempt to find some knowledge about the missing evidence in her memories, Lara agreed. And this time, Devon wanted her physically to walk through the night her father had been killed.

"We'll never have a better chance," he pointed out. "In a few hours, we'll be leaving here, and you can't come back until we can move against the cartel."

Lara understood that, and even though she didn't believe that the key lay in her memories, she was willing to try a last time for Devon's peace of mind.

The two agents who had remained were sent out of sight, and then Devon called Ching, carried him to the top of the stairs, and told him to stay there.

"I wondered why you brought him along," Lara commented, standing by the front door.

"He was here that night," Devon said, coming back down the stairs and moving to a position to the left of the front door. "Now, face the door with your hand on the switch. We can't make the place dark in the afternoon, but I want you to remember how it was that night."

"All right. It was dark. I was reaching for the light switch when Ching howled—"

"*Yarrr!*"

Lara hadn't noticed Devon send a brief hand signal to her cat, who had rapidly learned stage cues for the play, and the sudden howl sent a chill through her.

"Good Lord," she muttered. "How did you—"

"Shhh. I rehearsed with him while you were in the shower. Now concentrate, honey. You're reaching for the light switch, and then—" He signaled the cat again.

"*Yarrr!*"

Lara's fingers hesitated, then quickly flicked the light switch. She turned around, uneasy.

"Tell me what you're thinking," Devon ordered softly.

"I've never heard him sound like that before," she murmured. Her eyes lifted to the top of the stairs and found the cat sitting on the first tread. "He doesn't want to come down." A frown flitted across her face. "That's odd." Her gaze left the cat and went to a table in the foyer. "Everything's such a mess, newspapers on the floor—"

"Lara," Devon said.

She was still remembering that night. "Hmmm?"

"Look back at Ching."

She returned her gaze to the cat, and again a faint frown flitted across her expression.

"What is it?" Devon kept his voice very soft.

In a vague but conversational tone, Lara said, "Well, I just don't see why, that's all. The one he had was just fine, and almost new. Why change it?"

"What's different, Lara?"

"His collar," she answered obediently.

"What's wrong with it?"

"He's wearing a new one. It's darker against his fur, I can see that. Why would Dad get him a new collar when there was nothing wrong with his old one?"

Even as the puzzled words left her lips, Lara blinked, and a sudden chill snapped her out of the memories. "His collar," she whispered. "I haven't thought about it since . . ."

Devon took her hand. "Are you all right?"

"Yes, of course. Devon, the collar!"

"Ching," Devon called, leading Lara to the bottom of the stairs. The cat bounded down to meet them, bright-eyed and proud of himself for having flawlessly followed his idol's stage directions.

"Wauur?" he asked Devon.

"You're a smart cat," Devon told him, bending to unfasten the leather collar. "But I wish you'd been smart enough to tell us where to look all this time."

Ching gently bit his wrist.

"Sorry," Devon murmured. "We just didn't know the right question to ask, did we, boy?"

"Yah," Ching said.

Lara sat down on the third step, trying not to hope too much. "But, it's such a little thing! Devon, I might not even have noticed it. In fact, I hardly did. How on earth did you know?"

"I didn't." He sat on the step beside her and began examining the collar carefully. "But I had a hunch. The way you frowned when you remembered Ching from that night. You seemed to be bothered by more than the fact that he was upset. I thought it was worth a try."

Lara watched as he examined the silver bell and then detached it from the collar and set it aside. "But what could Dad have hidden in a collar? A message?"

"We'll find out." Devon studied the collar, which was made of two strips of leather stitched together, then produced a pocket knife and began prying gently at the stitches. He started at the pointed end of the collar, revealing the rough inner surface of the strips. He carefully cut more stitches. Then, just past the notch worn by the buckle of the collar, they both saw the edge of a strip of paper.

"I don't believe it!" Lara mumbled.

The other two agents had returned to the foyer, and both stood watching Devon work.

"You mean the cat had it all this time?" one of them exclaimed.

"Yah!" Ching said from his position on the fifth stair, disliking the term of address.

"Sorry, Ching," the man said absently.

She was so tense, she could hardly think; but Lara couldn't help smiling. Her cat made his feelings known so plainly that it no longer surprised her to hear even strangers react to him as if they understood him completely.

"It's a tight fit," Devon murmured, working very carefully to cut the stitches without disturbing what lay between them. "He must have had this already done that night, just in case."

Lara was watching intently. "There's something else. The paper's wrapped around something."

Devon cut the last stitch and gently removed the paper and what it enclosed. "A key." It was a tiny key, very narrow and flexible. He unfolded the strip of paper, and they could all see the neatly typed words.

The top of the safe, Lara.

Within seconds, they were all in her father's study.

Devon lifted down the painting that hid the safe; it had been mended, but the hinges were ruined, and so the painting had simply been hung on a hook.

"Wasn't this safe checked out?" Devon demanded of one of the agents.

"Of course it was. Some of them have false bottoms or backs, and we checked. Nothing."

"The top of the safe," Lara read from the message.

"You don't know what it means?" Devon asked her.

"No. I thought it was just a very obvious safe."

"What's the combination?"

Lara gave it to him and watched while he twisted the dial and opened the heavy door. The safe was empty, smooth walls giving nothing away. Devon began probing the inner surface with a careful, sensitive touch. Then he searched the facing where the door rested when it was closed. He closed it, examined the front minutely.

"Nothing." He stepped back and let his gaze roam slowly over the area. Above the safe was heavy pine paneling, the only wall in the room that was paneled. His eyes narrowed, and he stepped forward again to study the wall.

"Damn," he muttered softly.

"What is it? Have you found it?" Lara spoke tensely.

"This knot in the paneling. Wait a minute." He produced the tiny key and carefully inserted it in an all but invisible slot that, if noticed, would have looked like a simple and natural crack in the wood. And when he gave the key a quarter-turn clockwise, they heard the soft hum.

The paneling didn't open. Instead, the "very obvious" safe slid down out of sight behind the paneling, and another safe descended from inside the wall and took its place.

"We ought to be taking notes," one of the agents muttered. "Eliminate a false bottom or back, and who'd think there was another safe sitting on top of this one?"

Devon looked at the combination dial, then at Lara. "Your birthday. Month, day, year."

She gave him the numbers quickly, and the safe opened. Inside was the evidence. And it was more than any of them had expected. Notes, documents, diagrams. Some items were wrapped in plastic and marked clearly to indicate they bore important fingerprints—and those included two complete sets of stolen classified designs.

"We've got them," Devon said.

The following day, the newspapers carried hasty stories about a series of unexpected arrests by the FBI. Little information was available, they stated unhappily, but a number of highly influential people involved in the cutting edge of technology and the inner circles of government were involved. . . .

"They don't know what's going on," Lara said, pushing the newspaper off the bed.

"They will when the cartel goes to trial."

Lara turned to cuddle closer to Devon, folding her hands on his chest and smiling down at him. "Ching will get his feelings hurt if nobody happens to mention that he literally carried the key all this time."

They both heard newspaper being fiercely shredded on the floor by the bed.

"Can he read?" Devon asked.

"Do you really want to know?"

"No."

"Neither do I. But I do want to know why he was so hostile to Luke. Melanie is understandable, but—"

Devon kissed her. "Darling, that's the easiest answer of all. Let's get married quickly."

Lara allowed herself to be momentarily distracted. "I'd like that. But you and I are going to have trouble establishing residency for a license. Or will we?"

He grinned at her. "You and your cat have just aided the Federal Bureau of Investigation in toppling a criminal cartel that had infiltrated the highest levels of technology, to say nothing of a few scared government circles. Do you really think anybody's going to balk at waiving a simple little thing like establishing residency or a waiting period?"

Solemnly, she said, "You know, I never thought about it quite that way."

"I knew you were modest."

She kissed him, then said, "But I think we should go back to Pinewood after, and get on with the play. Nick would go to pieces if he had to replace us this late."

Devon sighed. "I was afraid you were going to suggest that. Well, since I don't have to wear tights, I suppose we can. Odd way to spend a honeymoon, though."

"I think it's perfect. After all, how many people get to spend their honeymoon in a fairy tale?"

"That is true."

Lara frowned at him. "And you distracted me. Why was Ching hostile to Luke?"

"He was also hostile to a couple of the other men in the stage crew, remember?"

"Sure, but—"

"What did they all have in common, Lara?"

She thought about it for a minute, then slowly began to smile. "Young. And handsome. Charming."

"Exactly. You said yourself that Ching's an excellent judge of character; he decided I was perfect for you and didn't want another man getting in the way. I'll bet when we go back to the theater, he'll be completely polite to Luke and the others."

And it turned out that Devon was right. When they showed up at the theater a few days later wearing matching wedding bands and a quite truthful tale of a whirlwind ceremony to explain their absence, Ching greeted Luke as an old and sincerely valued friend.

"I don't know what it is," Luke said in total bafflement, "but it isn't a cat!"

Epilogue

He studied several newspaper articles with a satisfied smile, then chuckled at a photocopy of a marriage certificate, before closing the file and setting it aside. He'd burn it later, since he no longer had any use for it, but for now he simply put it out of his way.

He reached out to the tidy stack of files and lifted the topmost one, opening it on the desk before him. In the golden circle of light provided by a shaded lamp, he studied the papers in the file thoughtfully. Difficult, he decided, but not impossible.

Impossible was a word he hadn't used in many years.

The personalities were fascinating, he thought. Not so many shadows this time, but some pain and a great deal of wariness. These two would no doubt fight each other all the way. That didn't disturb him; two flints would make a fire that would warm all the way to the soul.

If it didn't burn the house down first.

His long, elegant fingers searched through the papers, setting some aside and holding several for a close inspection. Slowly, a plan began to take shape in his keen brain.

The ball, of course. The man would be there, and so would the woman—the children would see to that. They'd been planning it for months, after all. They were an accomplished pair, and no mistake; one would think they'd been at this as long as he had. They had been very thorough in their schemes.

So was he.

He chuckled deep in his chest, a sound of utter delight. Drawing forward a lined pad, he made swift notes of observations to be made and answers to be found once he was on the scene, and arrangements to be dealt with.

"Now, then," he said softly to himself.

"Cy? Come to bed, darling."

Her voice evoked the response in him that was still wondrous and exhilarating even after all these decades; he could feel the warmth and joy spread through him, and he basked in it for a timeless moment of sheer enchantment. Was there, he wondered happily, anything more precious than a shared love so deep it enfolded the spirit in ageless delight? No. Nothing.

"Cyrus?"

"Coming, my sweet," he called.

The old man with an eternal spark of youth in his heart rose from the desk and left the comfortable library with the confident, eager steps of a man in love.

Coming next month . . .

HOT TOUCH
by Deborah Smith

Deborah Smith is one of LOVESWEPT'S brightest new stars. Her first LOVESWEPT published in March 1988 was on the bestseller list; her second was featured in the new author sampler and received rave reviews. With her irresistible wit, her incredibly steamy love scenes, and what *Romantic Times* has called "her refreshingly unique characters," Deborah Smith creates "must read" novels.

In **HOT TOUCH** Paul Belue, a temperamental Cajun veterinarian, owns a Louisiana plantation that's home to a veritable zoo of wildlife. When he leases his home and his pet wolf to a movie crew, he gets more entertainment than he bargained for. The producers hire elegant animal trainer Caroline Fitzsimmons to keep the wolf in line, but she soon finds that his owner is the one who needs taming as you will see from this excerpt of their first meeting.

"Sir, the lady says you'll have to move the alligator."

Paul stared down at the sweating, uncertain chauffeur. "The lady refuses to get out and walk, yes?"

"Uh, yes. She's not dressed for walking, see. And she doesn't like the heat."

Paul inhaled slowly, his fists clenching and unclenching. "Let me make certain before I do anything. This is Caroline Fitzsimmons, yes?"

"Uh, yes."

Narrowing his eyes, Paul looked at the limo and smiled. No Beverly Hills prima donna was going to meddle with his wolf. "I'll talk to the lady."

Caroline fidgeted, wondering what kind of crude, backward man blocked their way. To distract herself she fished through her Louis Vuitton travel bag and selected a pair of wraparound sunglasses with sleek silver frames. She put the glasses on and retrieved a gold compact from the bag.

She was checking her lipstick when her door was jerked open so hard that the limo rocked. Startled, Caroline dropped her compact and twisted quickly toward the invader.

"Haul your butt out of this car, chère!"

He had an incredibly deep voice. It was the voice of doom, if doom had a Cajun accent. Her mouth gaping, Caroline stared up at him.

He blocked the sun. He was big, or maybe he just seemed that way because he was so close. He wore only faded jeans and muddy, laced-up work boots, one of which he placed jauntily on the edge of her door like a challenge.

Caroline blinked rapidly and swallowed. Her mind took control of her gaping mouth and snapped it shut. She reached behind her on the seat, clasped a white umbrella with black polka dots, and brandished it at him like a club.

"I don't know what swamp you crawled out of, but go back to it," she ordered. "I'm here on business. You've obviously mistaken me for someone who enjoys the odor of sweat and dirt."

Muscles flexed in his brawny arms as he leaned forward. He flashed her a startlingly white smile. It had all the warmth of a dog's snarl. . . .